I DIDN'T KNOW

Costigan, the *Herald*'s editor, pulled the swing-gate open, gestured with a nod toward the chair pulled across the desk from his own and said, "Sit down, Will, and get it off your chest."

He crossed in front of Will, slapped his pants pockets for a match, then reached out to open the left-hand drawer.

Remembering that Costigan was left-handed, Will put out both arms and lunged, shoving. Off balance now, Costigan crashed into the side wall and fell to his knees. He picked up a wooden mallet from the floor beside him. "You must want your face made over, Will," Costigan taunted.

Will took a step toward him and pulled open the upper left-hand drawer. There, lying on a stack of paper, was Costigan's pistol. Will palmed it up, cocked it and said, "Throw the mallet away—and not at me."

Costigan brandished the mallet and smiled. "That gun's empty. You think I'm crazy enough to load it?"

"Then it won't hurt if I pull the trigger."

He did.

THE OUTRIDER

Luke Short

A Dell Book

Published by
Dell Publishing
a division of
Bantam Doubleday Dell Publishing Group, Inc.
666 Fifth Avenue
New York, New York 10103

ISBN: 0-440-20502-6

Reprinted by arrangement with the author's estate

Printed in the United States of America

Published simultaneously in Canada

January 1990

10 9 8 7 6 5 4 3 2 1

KRI

OUTRIDER

"One whose duty it is to ride about the range and keep a sharp lookout for anything that might happen to the detriment of his employer. While his duties are similar to the line rider's, unlike the line rider, who patrols a prescribed boundary, the outrider is commissioned to ride anywhere."*

*From *Western Words: A Dictionary of the Range, Cow Camp and Trail,* by Ramon F. Adams, University of Oklahoma Press, 1944.

1

The special train from upstate pulled slowly up to the Granite Forks depot platform, gave a last sigh and stopped in the bright early-morning sunlight.

From the three passenger coaches people began to descend. All—men, women and children—were dressed in somber clothes, and Will Christie, himself wearing an unaccustomed and uncomfortable dark suit, watched these members of the state legislature, mayors, town councilmen and plain ranchers with their wives and families, and wondered if he could spot his man. Thanks to some careful coaching, he did.

The man he approached through the crowd was less than his own height, tanned, slim, grey mustache below greyer eyes and black Stetson worn at a jaunty angle.

Will drew up beside him and said, "Mr. Cope?"

Brady Cope halted and looked at Will and said, "Yes." Then he added with friendly curiosity, "Do I know you?"

"No, sir," Will said, "Joe sent me to meet you. I'm Will Christie."

Cope extended his hand, smiling. "You're Joe's secretary. Glad to meet you, Will." He gave him an appraising glance, noting the wide shoulders, the soberness of his lean, weathered face that was belied by a hint of impudence in his blue eyes, and a high-bridged nose that had been broken and imperfectly set. Cope said, "You don't look like a secretary, Will. Joe must keep you outdoors, like a horse."

Will smiled, "I wish he did." He pointed with his chin, like an Indian, and said, "There's a hack out back. Any luggage?"

"No. The train goes back an hour after the funeral."

They walked through the rank of hack drivers who were calling for customers for the ride to the church and out to the cemetery. Will pointed to the waiting hack driver he had spoken for. He let Cope precede him into the hack and then directed the driver to the State House. As the hack started up, Cope asked, "How's Joe doing?"

Will hesitated a moment before he said, "I think he hurts all the time, but you'd never know it from him."

Cope nodded, but made no comment. As the hack crossed Front Street they could see past the driver to the high bluff on which the stone State Capitol looked down on the town this warm, clear fall morning. Its windows were brassily reflecting the sun.

The town of Granite Forks was basically a cowtown, built on a triangle of rolling land between two forks of the White River. Its bank and county courthouse were brick, but most of the buildings on Front Street and the side streets were frame, with false fronts built from lumber cut in the Sisters Range that shouldered up immediately to the west.

The hack horse labored up the hill through the residential section of small frame homes until the hack pulled up on the gravel drive before the Capitol steps. Will told the driver they would be inside half an hour or so, and then he and Cope climbed the broad steps of the three-story building, went through massive doors and turned left.

Will took a step ahead of Cope and opened a door which bore the legend in gilt, *Joseph M. Isom, Lieutenant Governor*.

Cope entered an anteroom which held two desks and a filing cabinet in front of a big window. Along both walls of the anteroom were leather-covered benches;

2

in the right wall was an open door, and Will said, "Go right in, Mr. Cope. He's waiting for you."

Brady took off his hat, revealing a thick shock of greying hair, and then stepped through the door into Isom's big office. He was just in time to see Joe Isom behind his big flat-topped desk lurching to his feet with the aid of a heavy cane.

Lieutenant Governor Joe Isom, black-haired, thirty-five years of age, dark-eyed, close to homely the way Abraham Lincoln was, and just as tall and gangling, limped around the corner of his desk, a wide smile of genuine welcome on his face. They met beside one of the two leather-covered chairs that faced the desk and shook hands. "It's great to see you, Brady," Isom said. "How long's it been?"

"Since the inaugural, Joe. You're looking fit enough."

Joe gestured to a chair, saying, "Sit down. How's the family?"

"Never better, thanks."

Before seating himself, Cope looked around the room, noting the bookcases along the far wall, a leather-covered sofa separating them, and then at the conference table flanked by half a dozen straight-backed chairs. With its huge flowered carpet and framed portraits of previous Lieutenant Governors, it was an altogether handsome room.

Cope gestured to the conference table and said, "Do you hold staff meetings like Billy Orr used to? If he couldn't fill all those chairs every morning he used to drag people in from the hall."

Joe limped across to the second heavy leather-covered chair, turned it a bit to face Cope's and while he was doing it said, "I've never held a conference, Brady. As far as I know, the only person who ever sat there is the cleaning woman when she wanted to rest her feet."

Cope smiled and both men sat down. Christie, who had followed Cope in, now moved toward the door.

"Will, will you please check next door for any news of the Governor?"

3

Will left the room, closing the door behind him. Isom said then, "We've got a little more than an hour before the funeral, Brady. I don't think it'll take that long for you to give me an answer—a kind of an answer, that is."

"To what, Joe?" Cope asked in a friendly sort of voice, his curiosity controlled.

"Brady, do you know you are looking at the Governor?"

Cope thought a few seconds, then said, "Sam Kilgore must be out of the state."

"He is, so I'm Acting Governor. He's somewhere in Montana on a hunting trip. His office and mine have been trying to reach him." He smiled faintly. "His office has been trying harder than mine."

"Why, Joe?"

Joe tucked his cane on the seat beside him before he said, "In a little more than an hour we'll be burying the late Attorney General Hugh Evans."

Cope nodded. "That's why I'm here, to honor a mighty tough enemy."

"That's why you're in Granite Forks. It's not why you're sitting here."

"No, that's in answer to your telegram, Joe. Why'd you want to see me?"

"For the simplest of reasons," Isom said quietly. "In Old Sam's absence, and as Acting Governor, I can appoint you Attorney General, Brady." He paused, then asked, "Do you want it? Would you take it?"

Both men regarded each other and for a full half-minute they were silent.

Then Cope spoke. "For your sake I don't think I should, Joe. If you appointed me, Old Sam would make it a point of honor to destroy you. I've fought him since we were a territory. You couldn't appoint a man more hostile to him than I am."

"Exactly," Joe said. He leaned forward and said soberly, "There's nothing Old Sam can do to me that he hasn't done already. This State House gang is a closed corporation, Brady—closed to me. Old Sam

4

goes around me or over me, but never through me. I've had more people in my waiting room this past week than've been in it since the inauguration. When Old Sam gets back I'll be able to shoot deer in it again."

Cope only smiled and shook his head and Joe went on. "He's got the leaders of both houses in his pocket, along with the chairmen of all the important committees. But most important of all, he had a tame, tough and smart Attorney General in Hugh Evans. If the mining boys or the railroad people wanted anything, Old Sam would tell Hugh to see they got it."

Cope nodded. "What you really mean is they never got what they didn't want."

"That puts it better," Joe conceded. He spread his hands, shrugged and leaned back in his chair. "I'm a showpiece, Brady. I got elected by a fluke, and we both know it."

Brady smiled faintly. "It's not every election we can vote in a certified hero."

"A newspaper hero," Joe scoffed. "As a captain of the Rangers I was doing exactly what I was paid to do—break up a rustling ring. If that shootout hadn't happened, I would still be a captain of the Rangers."

"But tied to a desk, shuffling papers, Joe. No, don't poor-mouth it."

"All right, but it's beside the point, Brady. You haven't answered my question. Do I appoint you Attorney General or don't I? The Attorney General's office has almost unlimited power. Mine has none—except to name you Attorney General. And it's got to be quick."

"Damn!" Cope said. "I'll be leaving a wife, a son and a daughter upstate for a room in a hotel swarming with jackleg politicians. I'll be leaving my cows for these Capitol pigs. I'll be leaving my practice to prosecute malpractice."

Isom smiled faintly, but said nothing.

Then Cope shrugged. "I'll take it. Not that I want it, but there's a house-cleaning to do."

Isom rose and was shaking hands with Cope when a soft knock came on the anteroom door. It was opened and Will Christie stepped in.

"No contact with Old Sam, boss. Maybe somebody shot him."

"No, we can't have everything," Isom said drily, then added, "Congratulate our new Attorney General, Will. Then find out if Judge Bates is in, will you, please?"

Smiling, Will shook hands with Cope, congratulating him, and said to Isom, "I just saw Judge Bates unlocking his office door."

Isom looked at Cope. "Let's get you sworn in, Brady."

2

Although Will was dressed for the funeral of Hugh Evans he did not attend. Joe had agreed that since the Governor was out of the state and his staff and most of the State House crowd would be attending the funeral, someone had to keep the store.

At his desk in the anteroom Will shucked out of his coat and from the bookcase behind his desk took out a casebook borrowed from the law library upstairs and opened it to the marker slip he had left in it. On the theory that since his title was Legislative Assistant to the Lieutenant Governor, he ought to know some law. He did know some, but he needed to know more, and the more was what he was after before he could even attempt to pass the state bar examination.

As he sat down he wondered what arguments Joe had marshaled that persuaded Brady Cope to accept the Attorney Generalship. Joe, he remembered, had not been optimistic about Cope's willingness to accept the office. Joe had never said it, but Will knew he thought it. It was, Will reflected, typical of Joe Isom's way of thinking—you expected nothing and hoped for everything.

As he flipped open the casebook, he wondered how Joe would get through the ride to the cemetery, the long ceremony and the ride back to the train and to here. If it wouldn't have seemed an impropriety and undignified, Joe could have ridden his horse to the funeral, for he could and often did ride. By some quirk of the healing process in Joe's battered body it was less painful for him to ride than to sit or to walk. Joe would make out all right today because he always did; he was as truly indestructible as any man Will had ever known.

In thinking that, he recalled most of the details of the fight that had crippled Joe. He even remembered their first meeting in Joe's basement office in the old brick Capitol building that was now the Granite Forks county courthouse.

As a young brand inspector working for the Cattlemen's Association in the southern part of the state, Will had come across evidence of both horse and cattle brands being altered. What had started out as a more or less routine investigation turned out to be what could only be called a conspiracy involving more than two dozen rustlers and drifters from Texas and up from Mexico. It was a bigger job than the Cattlemen's Association could handle. Because Will had uncovered it he was the Association's emissary to Captain Joe Isom of the State Rangers.

In his hot basement office, Isom had listened to Will's story with initial reserve, and subsequently with friendly interest. As Will laid out the details and the

7

names of many of the men involved, Isom realized that Will was onto a big rustling ring that was shipping cattle with altered brands and forged bills of sale, not south into the cheap markets of Mexico but north to the commission houses in Kansas City.

It took some time and some undercover work on Isom's part to pinpoint the center of the operation. It was a huge ranch close to the town of Tres Piedras in the southern part of the state, in the brushy country where cattle hid themselves and literally had to be dragged out into an open space where their brands could be read. This was big country, most of it leased for next to nothing under a dozen different names and brand registrations.

When Isom, with all the rangers that could be spared him, moved in on the operation they first struck at the isolated line camps, picking up some men, losing others, but word of their activities got to the headquarter ranch at Tres Piedras. When it came to the raid on the big collection of adobe buildings there, Isom, Will, and the remaining six rangers laid siege.

It took a day and a night of exchanging gunfire before Isom realized they were not only outnumbered and outgunned, but very close to being driven off. On the evening of the second day Isom decided to give up his waiting game. Under cover of darkness, he moved his men closer to the big house and placed them in sheltered locations, and by himself he moved quietly toward the big dark house. When the rangers heard the barrage of gunfire erupting inside the house, they were sure Isom had made it inside and they charged the house from four sides.

In the shootout that followed the rangers were certain of only one thing; Joe had entered the main room. What few glass windows were in the house had been shattered. The rangers piled inside and it turned out to be mostly sound shooting, for there were no lights in the house except the light cast by a screened fire in the big room. When the rangers, Will still with them, converged on the room they found five dead men whom only Isom could have shot; the six other men who had fled to the big room were captured. Isom, lying between two of his dead assailants, seemed to be dead himself. His body, by later account, had taken seven bullets, and it was Will who discovered that Isom was still alive.

And it was Will with one of the rangers who by lantern light hitched up the wagon and loaded Isom into it. Tres Piedras had, it turned out, a Mexican-American doctor who spoke only Spanish. They were guided to him by one of the crowd who had gathered out of gun range to watch the two-day shootout.

While Will stayed with Isom in Tres Piedras, the rangers had headed north for the railroad with their captives. The news of the fight had spread and the rangers were stopped by a posse of angry cattlemen who, at gunpoint, took two of the rustlers and hanged them.

The news of the gunfight spread across the state and beyond it, and Joe Isom soon became a kind of folk hero. When he was able to be moved, he was taken by train to the Granite Forks four-bed hospital in the home of Doctor Price, and here he was bedeviled daily for a short period by newspapermen. For some reason Will could never fathom, newspapers and magazines in the East picked up the story and sensationalized it. They said, in effect, that this was the wildest of the West, with an authentic hero as its central figure.

Joe's convalescence was slow and painful, and when it was certain that he would be pensioned off as being physically unfit to qualify as a ranger the politicians stepped in. They persuaded him to run against the Lieutenant Governor in the election coming up. He won office handily but Will knew that Joe, who had hired him as his secretary the day after his victory was announced, was as restless, dissatisfied and frustrated as he himself was. The fact of the matter was that Joe was honored everywhere, and consulted by no one.

Before he put his attention on the casebook Will

wondered how the news of Cope's appointment would be greeted by Old Sam.

An hour later the swelling racket of footsteps in the corridor told him the funeral was over. He put his notes in the casebook, rose, and was putting the book back on the shelf when the door to the anteroom was opened. He turned and saw a squat, half-bald man, coatless and tieless, amble in, a wet, dead cigar in the corner of his big, wide mouth. This was Phil Costigan, editor and publisher of the *Granite Forks Herald*. His shirt was collarless and dirty, and his hands were ink-stained.

"Your boss in?" Costigan asked in a surly voice as he halted in front of Will's desk.

"No," was Will's short reply.

Will looked past Costigan's shoulder and through the door the editor had left open, and saw Isom pass in the corridor headed toward his office that opened onto the corridor.

"I stand corrected," Will said. "He just came in. Take a seat."

Will crossed over to the office door, knocked and stepped inside. Joe had already taken off his coat, loosened his tie and was limping toward the desk. Will let him seat himself before he said, "Phil Costigan is outside, Joe. Want to see him?"

Isom scowled. "No, but I suppose I'll have to. Show him in, and stay here, Will."

Will opened the door, said curtly, "Come in, Phil," and stood aside.

An impatient Phil Costigan strode in, made for Isom's desk and sat on the corner of it looking at Isom.

"I just thought of something," Costigan said. "Your initials are J. I. They wouldn't stand for Judas Iscariot, would they?"

From just inside the closed door Will said, "Justice Invincible, Phil."

Isom made no attempt to shake hands with Costigan and Costigan didn't expect him to. He ignored Will.

10

The editor said, "You think you'll get away with this, Joe?"

"I already have," Isom said drily.

"What if I printed I saw Old Sam yesterday over in Socaton? What if I printed the names of five other men who saw him too? What if I proved he was in the state?"

"Go ahead," Isom said carelessly. "Only your readers will wonder why your six men didn't bother to tell Sam his Attorney General was dead. They'll also wonder why he didn't come to the funeral." Isom shook his head, "No, Phil, try something else."

"You don't deny you're a traitor to your boss?" Costigan snarled.

"I don't have a boss, Phil, except my conscience."

"He put you on the ticket. Deny that if you can."

"I won't try. All this hero stuff they were printing about me and he was saying about me was just a trick, Phil. Like a card sharp making you watch one of his hands while he's cheating you with the other," Isom said.

"I never thought you were a hero," Costigan said sourly.

Isom smiled. "You know, I never did either." Now he leaned his elbows on the desk. "Go away, Phil. I've got people to see."

Costigan came to his feet. He removed the dead cigar from his mouth, revealing a chewed-up cud of tobacco the size of a child's fist. His dark eyes were hard.

"All right, Joe. You declared the war. If you or Brady Cope ever get a friendly word from the *Herald* it'll be because I missed it. And I don't miss."

"Good-bye, Phil. Forever, I hope," the Lieutenant Governor said.

"No, it won't be forever, you crooked bastard. I'll be on your neck from now on."

Will moved over to stand beside Joe. "I'll do it, Joe. I'm closer," he said.

Isom nodded. "Not too hard," he said.

Will took a step toward Costigan and swung. He caught the middle of Costigan's soft belly with his fist and the force of the blow knocked Costigan into the desk and onto the floor.

Ignoring him, Will walked the length of the room, opened the corridor door and came back. Costigan was massaging his belly now and he came to his feet to face Will.

"Out," Will said.

"You wait," Costigan said, his voice hoarse with anger. Followed by Will, he tramped across the room and went through the doorway, leaving it open.

Twin Buttes was a lead- and silver-mining town seventy miles south of Granite Forks. It was an ugly tangle of shacks, tents and frame buildings, some of two stories. The wide main street, flanked by grimy false-front stores and rooming houses, ended and splintered just beyond the railroad tracks into roads that led to a jungle of head frames, hoist shacks, ore bins and high-stack smelters and reduction mills.

The miners were streaming from the mines that pocked the face of gaunt Twin Buttes Mountain immediately to the west, for it was a change of shift. As the last of them hit the flats several sporadic rumbles of powder blasts could be heard. These would provide the ore for the night shifts to muck out while the drillers double-jacked holes on the new faces.

In minutes the town and its saloons were aswarm with miners, the weary day shifts wanting drinks and food, the night shifts fortifying themselves for their coming labor. Huge high-wheeled ore wagons from distant mines knifed through the traffic on their way to mill or smelter.

It was full dark, the night shifts already at work, when a distant rumble from Twin Buttes Mountain was audible in the town. It was of long duration and gently shook the earth. If it had been day instead of night the town could have seen the plume of dust that gushed out the tunnel at Number 4 level of the Mary E.

Presently, four lamps in single file descended in a hurried zigzag. Only seconds after they reached the Mary E's engine house a hoarse-throated steam whistle began to bray the short, long, short, long signal over and over that was the agreed upon call for help. At the same time it announced disaster.

3

Brady Cope shoved his plate away from him, packed his pipe and lit it while his daughter brought a cup of coffee from the stove and set it on the kitchen table before him. She took his plate and joined her mother at the sink.

Belle, his daughter, was taller than her mother, but she had the same straight nose, blue eyes and generous mouth. Where Janet's hair was as shot with grey as his, Belle's was a soft chestnut color, and curling. Her face was tanned and she had a healthy glow.

Both women decided at the same time that they were finished cleaning up. As if they'd rehearsed it, they took off their aprons with identical movements and hung them up on a cabinet doorknob.

Janet reached the table first and said, "Let's sit out here. The stove feels good." She sat down and moved the lamp against the wall.

Brady waited until Belle, smoothing out the bodice of her navy blue dress, came over and took the third chair. Both mother and daughter had eaten supper hours ago, knowing Brady's funeral train would reach Meredith late, which it had.

Brady took the pipe from his mouth and, holding it in his hand, said, "Well, I've told you all who were at the funeral as close as I can remember. I even described the ladies' dresses. But something else happened today."

"At the funeral?" his wife asked.

"No. Before." He looked fondly at them both before he said, "As of around nine-thirty this morning you have been, respectively, the wife and daughter of the state's new Attorney General."

Janet looked first at him, then imploringly at the ceiling, and said, "Brady Cope, you are *the* most maddening man who ever lived! You've let us chatter like idiots—you, you lawyer!" She laughed, rose and leaned over and kissed him. "I'm sorry we fed you. I'd send you to bed, only I want to know what happened."

So Brady told them of his early-morning meeting with Joe Isom and of the circumstances that allowed his very proper and legal appointment.

When he had finished Belle said thoughtfully, "I'm not sure I like that, Pa. It seems so—well, almost sneaky and underhanded."

"Oh, absolutely. But, legal."

Janet asked, "But, Brady, this means you're part of Sam Kilgore's machine. Can you live with that?"

"It means I'm not part of Old Sam's machine," Brady said flatly. "I'm the foot in the door, and a pretty big foot. He can't fire me. He can yell for an investigating committee, but he's too coony for that. No, he's got to live with me and he's not going to like it, I promise you."

"Oh, dear," Janet said softly. "After two terms in the Senate I thought you were fed up with politics. You said you were."

"I was one vote of the minority party. Surely, you can see this is different."

14

"How is it, Pa?" Belle asked.

Brady thought a moment. "Well, I'm lawyer for the state. I'm supposed to see state laws enforced."

"Doesn't sound very exciting. You'd be just a sheriff without a gun, wouldn't you, Pa?"

Cope nodded, smiling. "I never heard it put that way, but, yes. There's more though. The key men in the legislature can be bought. The railroad is buying up banks, then borrowing the depositors' funds at almost no interest. The mines are fighting any sort of state control over safety regulations and working conditions. Those are just a few of the things I'll aim to take on."

Janet, who had been eyeing him speculatively, said now, "Brady, how much time do we have to move?"

"You and Belle are not moving to Granite Forks," Brady said flatly. "You hated living there while I was in the Senate. Both of you can stay here on the ranch. Have Bill and Marion move in here so there'll be a man around the house. Bill can ride into the office, just as I do."

"But where will you stay in Granite Forks?" Janet asked.

"At a hotel or boarding house, just like most of the fellows in the legislature."

"Pa, I was away at school when you were in the Senate. I've never lived there and I'd like it, I think."

Brady frowned. "What are you getting at?"

"Leave mother here with Bill and Marion. I'll go with you and we'll find a house and set up house-keeping."

Brady started to shake his head when Janet spoke up, "Do it, Brady. You can't live in a hotel room and eat just anywhere. You'd be sick after a month of it and you know it."

Brady looked at Belle appraisingly. "Would you really like it, Belle? You'd be town-bound for a long time."

"I've been ranch-bound for quite a spell. Yes, Pa, I'd really like it."

4

"The thing to do," Governor Sam Kilgore said, looking down at his glass of bourbon and water, "is exactly nothing, Frank."

This was said in answer to Frank Jackson's question of how he was going to retaliate against Joe Isom for his appointment of Brady Cope. It had been asked by a thin, bald and freshly sunburned man across the table of the private railway car he had provided for the Governor's hunting trip. Like the Governor, he was dressed in comfortable range clothes.

Sam Kilgore—Old Sam to friend and enemy alike—was a massive man but not fat; his big bones were just very solidly fleshed. A shock of thick dead-white hair over a broad, pleasantly pugnacious face bisected by a full white mustache gave him an air of benign blue-eyed impressiveness that he traded on shamelessly.

He took a swallow of his drink, then looked out the train window at the brown rolling grassland dotted with fat cattle that would soon be shipped. He did not really see them, for he was remembering yesterday evening.

Filthy, beard-stubbled and tired, but happy with the success of their hunt, they had picked up their mail at the hotel desk and climbed to the suite he was sharing with Frank, who was vice president of the Rocky Mountain Central Railroad.

Sam had told Frank to take the first crack at the bathtub while he read his mail, which turned out to be mostly telegrams. Without reading them he put them in chronological order, then read them, starting with the message from his secretary telling of Hugh Evans' death and the date of the funeral. He had felt a deep pang of regret at losing an old friend and he had wondered with quiet despair how he could do without him. Afterwards, he had read the dozen or so telegrams from his office and from the Senate leader, pleading with him to get in touch, to come back to name Evans' successor.

Then had come the bombshell—Joe Isom's telegram saying that as Acting Governor he had appointed Brady Cope Attorney General.

At first Sam had almost choked with rage at this treachery, but long before Frank had shaved and bathed he had control of himself and was even reflective. Why shouldn't Isom have stabbed him in the back with this appointment? He had treated Isom as he would an idiot child, circumventing him always, never trusting him with any confidences. Isom was a frank, independent maverick without a power base, a shot-up ex-ranger whose feats had made the state proud. Why, he himself had praised Joe from border to border of the state, hoping his laudatory speeches about him would win some votes, and they had. He had taken the telegrams into the bathroom and put them where Frank could reach them from the tub.

Frank's voice had interrupted his brooding in the bedroom. "You know, Sam, I don't see how four men as smart as we think we are could have been so damned dumb. If we'd only sent a packer back to town with word we'd changed our hunting grounds this never would have happened."

Old Sam had taken a pull on his drink and wiped his mustache. "That was why we went hunting, wasn't it? To get away from telegrams, desks and people, and do a little shootin' and drinkin'. Besides, what could happen at home—except what did?"

Now Frank rose, glass in hand, bracing himself against the lurch of the car. He looked at Sam's drink and asked, "Want that darkened?" At Sam's palm-out gesture of no, Frank went over to the bar cabinet. On its counter were the dregs of the drinks left half an hour ago by the two other members of the hunting party, who were put down at a spur where men with horses met them.

Frank mixed his own drink, then returned to the table. After sitting down, he asked. "What does Joe do for women, Sam? Think we could slip one in from out of state that could get to him?"

The Governor, who seldom gave anyone a flat no, pretended to think of this a moment, and said, "Possibly, Frank, but is it worth the trouble? He's done his damage, so let's forget him. It's Brady Cope that bothers me."

"Yeah, me too." Frank paused, then said with some bitterness, "When he didn't try for the Senate a third time I thought his tail was down. Now Joe's given him what he always wanted—a club to beat us with."

"He can't prove much against your people. There's no law says you can't contribute to a political party. Besides, most of it was in cash, and that's invisible."

"So, he can't hurt us, but can he hurt you?"

Sam finished his drink before replying in a remarkably cheerful tone of voice. "Yes, I am afraid he can, Frank. Not directly, but through men I've appointed and men they've appointed or hired. It all winds up in my lap." He rose now. "I could use a short nap before we get in, Frank. I don't know what I'll be meeting and I am damned tired."

He moved toward the back of the car, a walking bear of a man, and lay down in a lower berth.

An hour later what he met at the Granite Forks depot confused him for more than a moment. There were his middle-aged secretary, Ed Poland, and his young assistant, Fred Estey, waiting for him on the platform as he stepped down from the car ahead of Frank Jackson. There were a few people on the platform moving toward the coach ahead of them.

Beyond these people were Joe Isom and Will Christie talking to Brady Cope. Cope and Christie both had valises at their feet, which meant they hadn't come to meet him but were taking the train south. All three were wearing casual range clothes and worn Stetsons, he noted as he moved toward his secretaries to shake hands.

Once all had said hello, Sam said to Jackson and the secretaries, "Frank, you and I'd better go greet my new Attorney General."

As Old Sam approached them, Jackson trailing, Joe and Brady halted their conversation. Sam extended his huge hand to Cope first. "Congratulations, Brady. Joe made the choice I'd have made if I'd been here. Good to have you with us."

Cope only smiled and nodded, accepting the congratulations from Jackson.

The Governor shook hands with Joe and Will; then, careful to keep his real feelings from showing in his eyes, he said, "Good thinking, Joe. Brady and me have had our go-arounds but he's the best lawyer in the state, or in any other state."

"That's what I've always thought, too," Isom said drily.

Now Old Sam looked down at the valises and gestured loosely. "Where you fellows headed?"

He looked from one to the other, but it was Joe Isom who answered. "You haven't heard, Sam?"

"I haven't heard anything, as you damn well know. What is it?"

"Last night down at Twin Buttes there was a cave-in at the Mary E mine. They think between twenty and twenty-five men were trapped. They've already recovered five very dead bodies. More to come, Sam," Joe said.

Old Sam shook his head slowly, his eyes closed. "How goddamn awful," he said softly. He turned, took a few steps away from them, paused for a minute, then returned and wiped genuine tears from his eyes. "You're headed there, I take it?" he asked Joe.

"Just Brady and Will. I loaned Will to Brady because he hasn't got a staff yet."

19

Old Sam said to Brady, "Give them my deepest sympathy, will you?"

Joe said, "I already have, Sam. I telegraphed them in your name because I knew you'd want to yourself."

"I would have. Thanks, Joe." Old Sam looked at Brady now, a faint show of concern on his face. "I sort of hoped I could spend a couple of hours with you today, Brady. Can't you send Will instead of going yourself?"

"I don't think so, Sam. It's up to my office to investigate and prosecute, so I should see it first-hand. Will is my witness."

"Prosecute exactly what?" Old Sam demanded.

"I won't know that until I look around down there," Brady answered.

The engine's bell tolled discreetly as if to remind the two remaining passengers on the platform that even if they were talking to the Governor there was still a train to move.

Old Sam took the hint. He backed aside saying, "Let me know what's happening." Both passengers picked up their valises, nodded good-bye and headed for the coach steps. Brady Cope was first on and he took the first empty seat. Will followed, tossed his valise in the overhead rack and sat down beside him.

As the train started to move, Will said, "Old Sam knows what you're after, Mr. Cope."

Cope looked at him. "Make that Brady from now on, Will." Then he said, "Certainly he does. Know where the Mary E gets its name?" Will shook his head and Brady said, "It's the first name and middle initial of Mary Elizabeth Hatcher, the dead wife of Clay Hatcher. He owns the mine. He's also the largest stockholder of the railroad we're now riding on, and an old friend of Sam's. I was about to say, old friend and co-conspirator. The last I've got to prove."

Old Sam somberly watched the train pull out, waved good-bye to Isom, who headed for his hack; then he joined Jackson, who had heard and watched this. The station agent pulling the baggage cart halted his load

20

by them. The Governor and Jackson pointed out the saddles, guns, bedrolls and duffel bags and trophy racks belonging to them, and the two secretaries began toting all the gear to the hack drawn up alongside the platform.

Old Sam gestured with a movement of his head; Jackson nodded and together they moved down the platform out of earshot.

Sam halted and asked, "What do you think, Frank? Trouble maybe?"

They looked in each other's eyes before Old Sam said, "It ain't good."

Frank looked puzzled. "But what can Brady do to you, Sam?"

"Well, if you recall when he was in the Senate he used to bleed for the miners. This is ammunition for him."

Jackson moved close to the Governor and, tapping him gently on his broad chest, said with confidence, "Sam, his old bill was licked. It always will be licked. You said it once, so say it again: A man can do anything with his property he wants so long as he doesn't break the law. What law did the Mary E break?"

"None that I know of."

"All right. I feel sorry for those miners, but nobody marched them into the Mary E at gunpoint. Everybody knows mines are dangerous, even the dumbest hunkie mucker. Still, they took the jobs."

Old Sam gave a nod and a quiet sigh of resignation, or acceptance. "So, Joe sent a telegram to them down there. He signed my name. I'll tell Costigan I sent Cope to see if help was needed. That ought to look all right in print."

The two secretaries came toward them across the platform. Old Sam shook hands with Frank, saying, "Thanks for everything, Frank."

"My pleasure. And don't worry about Cope. Let's see what he comes up with."

Frank watched them climb into the hack and then

went inside the depot and stepped into the agent's office.

"Looks like you had a good hunt," the agent said.

Jackson nodded. "The best, Jess." He paused, then asked, "Anything new from Twin Buttes?"

"Yeah. It came through just as your train was pulling in. Twenty-one dead. They've reached the face, so that's all there are. They buried them as they found them on account of it's hot down there. But there'll be a mass funeral service tomorrow."

Jackson was silent a moment, then said soberly, "Rough." At Jess's nod Frank said quietly, "I reckon I'd starve before I'd work in a mine."

"Well, starving is a quicker way to die, but not by much," Jess observed.

Frank's office suite was on the second floor of a trim brick building across Front Street, opposite the station. A wrought-iron staircase led up to a half-glassed door that opened onto a corridor running the width of the building. The first door on the right was marked *Private*. The second door had on it the gilded legend, *Rocky Mountain Central R. R.* In the lower corner was the word *Welcome*.

He tried the door, found it locked, drew out his keys and unlocked it. It opened onto a reception room with easy chairs and his secretary's desk in the far corner. Crossing the room, he entered his own office, the one marked Private.

It was a luxurious room with full carpeting. In its center was a huge, low table surrounded by six easy chairs covered in fawn-colored leather, for it was here he entertained the politicians he hoped to influence. In the corridor corner was a glass-doored liquor cabinet and he headed for it. He poured himself a glass of whiskey, and holding it in his hand, he walked to the big front window and looked down at the street.

His mind was scheming as he remembered Isom's words to Old Sam, *"I loaned Will to Brady because he hasn't got a staff yet."* Apparently, Old Sam saw no significance in that or he would have mentioned it to

22

him, and Frank was glad of that. Old Sam must stay out of this. What it meant, though, was that in Brady's absence in Twin Buttes the Attorney General's office, still staffless, would be empty tomorrow.

And in that office, Frank knew, was a double-locked file cabinet. Hugh Evans had always kept the keys to the files on his watch-chain keyring. Frank was sure of that, for whenever he had brought any papers from the Central to Hugh—agreements that must be legalized but not made public—Hugh would read them, sign them if necessary and file them in the locked file cabinet. Hugh had been Old Sam's state party chairman and collector of party finances, and an honest one. Still, those locked files contained political dynamite for Sam. If they remained in the office, sooner or later Brady Cope would get around to having them opened. But if they weren't there, he couldn't open them, could he?

How to get them out? Sipping his drink, still looking out the window, his thoughts probed the possibilities. He discarded all of them, and then suddenly it came to him, so obvious he had overlooked it.

He finished his drink, let himself out into the corridor, sought the street and started walking the two blocks to the Granite Forks House.

The white-painted two-story hotel with a wide veranda the length of it was the politicians' hangout when the legislature was in session. Now, with the legislature still out but convening in ten days, the thirty barrel chairs strung along the veranda were empty. There were a few people in the big carpeted lobby waiting for other people. The small bar at the left side of the lobby, however, was crowded, for this was the drinking hour.

Frank paused in the saloon's doorway, looking at the drinkers bellied up to the bar and at the men seated at the four gaming tables. He spotted his man at the far end of the bar, apparently alone. Frank crossed the room and slipped in beside him. The younger man, wearing steel-rimmed glasses, fat, soft, with a balding head of blond hair, had seen him approach in the back-bar mirror and now he turned, extended a pudgy hand and said, "Where you been, Frank? All the girls in town are asking about you."

"I know only two girls, and neither of them would miss me, Cato."

This was Cato Jones, Hugh Evans' deputy and therefore Assistant Attorney General, a young lawyer who looked like a studious undertaker in his black suit and string tie. He always explained his unusual first name by saying that his father had chosen it because it set him apart from all the other Joneses.

"What are you drinking?" Cato asked.

"Whiskey and a little water. I'm paying for it, and for your refill, too."

"Um," Cato said, "that smells of bribery."

"It is, and it'll taste of it too. Let's take our booze out on the porch where we can talk alone." Frank ordered, and when they had their drinks they carried them through the lobby. Out on the veranda Frank led the way to the last two chairs, farthest from the lobby door.

When they were seated, Frank told of his hunting trip with Old Sam. While the hunting was a success, the news awaiting them of Hugh's death and Isom's appointment of Cope was an irretievable disaster. Cato agreed.

"Have you seen your new boss?" Frank asked.

Cato nodded. "Yesterday, but he's not my boss, Frank. We had a long and pleasant talk. The gist of it was that he wanted his own people in the office. I don't blame him. In his place I'd do the same thing. If he kept me Old Sam would have a spy in the office. He didn't say that, but I'm sure that's his thinking." Cato had a soft, pleasant voice, a lawyer's voice.

They drank, and then Frank asked, "What are your plans?"

"Haven't any. Set up shop here, maybe."

"That's a good idea. We can help. Once you're set we can throw a lot of work your way."

"You mean that?" Cato asked, seeming genuinely surprised.

"Well, somebody's got to buck Cope. You'll have all Sam's legal business and a lot more. And you won't be a pigeon, because you won't hold public office. Think it over."

"I've thought it over, and the answer is yes," Cato said promptly. "Let's drink to it."

When they had drunk, Frank was silent, letting Cato relish his prospects. Then he got down to the business he'd come for.

"Did Cope ask you for your office keys?"

"Why, no. I told him I'd clean out my stuff as soon as I could get around to it and he said there wasn't any hurry." He frowned. "Why'd you ask that, Frank?"

"Do you know where Cope is now and will be tomorrow?" When Cato shook his head, Frank said, "Twin Buttes, so his office will be empty up until train time tomorrow."

Cato nodded. "You've got something in mind, sounds like."

"I have." Jackson set his drink on the floor, leaned forward, elbows on knees, and clasped his hands together. "Those locked files of Hugh's."

Cato frowned. "You want me to break into them?"

His tone of voice had a wariness in it that made Frank laugh. "Anything but. I want you to start cleaning out your desk tomorrow morning. Two men will come in with authorization to take those files. They're in Hugh's office. Is it locked?"

"No. Hugh gave that up a long time ago. If he'd locked his office and we wanted something from his files we might wait half a day before he'd come back to let us in. Finally he threw the key away."

Frank nodded, reached down for his drink and finished it.

Cato looked at him appraisingly. "Can the men who pick up the files be recognized or traced?"

Frank came to his feet. "They're railroad workers.

25

They'll get on the train Brady gets off of. Anything else?"

"Where do the files go?"

Frank smiled and asked, "You don't really want to know that, do you?"

Cato eyed him thoughtfully and finally said, "No, I guess not."

5

On the blazing hot morning of the mass funeral services Twin Buttes was in an ugly mood. By order of the mayor all saloons were closed until after the services. The miners made no pretense of going to work and they milled aimlessly in the hot sunglare, forming angry groups that dissolved while other equally angry groups formed.

Will and Cope had agreed the night before in the double room of their shabby hotel that Will would attend the service in the Catholic Church and Cope the one in the Protestant Chapel. The two churches, the desk clerk told them, almost faced each other across Main Street.

Both men started together at nine-thirty to make sure they had seats. Both had agreed last night that, much as they hated to, they should attract some attention, showing that the state honored these humble miners even if the mine owners didn't.

They parted, and Will saw that his grimy frame church was larger than the church Brady was headed for. Inside, Will took a seat on the side aisle and watched the oven-hot church quickly fill. There were few women attending, and they were of two kinds. There were the plain, sturdy women who took the front benches closest to the altar. Then there were the whores who collected in the back row. As the church filled with miners, the stink of sweat, sour clothes, unwashed bodies and stale alcohol was so overpowering that Will breathed through his mouth.

Through the service Will was aware that he was being covertly watched. These red-eyed men, the sweat from their rescue attempt and the grave digging barely dry on their bodies, were wondering who this clean, well-dressed man in their midst could be, Will knew.

After the service he headed for the hotel. The miners who had filled the churches and gathered on the street in front of them headed downstreet for the saloons, which would now be open. He was watched on the street as he had been in the church, but now more openly, and with no friendliness.

Cope was sitting in a rickety chair on the hotel veranda. Will took the chair next to him and asked, "How was yours?"

"My people were mad," Brady said.

"So were mine."

"They know we're here. The minister thanked us. Did your priest?"

"Not unless he thanked us in Latin," Will said.

Cope smiled and stood up. "Well, if Superintendent Magruder got my note, he's waiting for me at the Mary E. I'd better get along."

"Sure you don't want me along?"

"I'm sure, Will. As I told you last night, if we both brace him he'll figure we're ganging up on him and he'll clam up. He'll figure you'll be my witness to anything he says. If I go in alone and ask just what happened and why, there's a chance he'll tell me." He leaned over and picked up his Stetson from the empty chair beside him, put it on and regarded Will again.

"You see," Cope continued, "he knows damned well

he hasn't violated anything on the books, because there's nothing on the books to violate. And whatever he says to me he can deny he said it. His word against mine, so it's a standoff."

"What if Sam's got the word to him not to see you?"

"That's possible." He passed in front of Will, then halted. "Mix around, Will. Just see how mad those miners are. Talk with them. Oh, Phil Costigan's in town. I saw him at the church."

Will only shrugged and watched Cope walk away. He looked out at the street and saw the miners filing into the saloons across the way. Something was missing, but what was it? And then he knew. Among all these men there were only a couple of horses in sight. Well, that figured. The mines owned the horses that hauled the ore, and on a miner's wages you couldn't afford a horse or the feed for it.

Now he rose, went up to his room, changed out of his white shirt into a denim one, left his coat and went outside. He crossed the wide street and went through the swinging doors of the Bullseye Saloon and found himself in a huge, crowded and very noisy room. He stepped away from the doors and halted, waiting for his eyes to adjust to the half-darkness. The bar was a long one and was crowded; along the wall to the right were benches packed with men; the four big round card tables were not covered with felt, but were bare, and the stools around them, all occupied, were solid sections of railroad ties, too heavy to throw easily. Will noted all this and more too. Heavy wire screening protected the inside of all four street windows and there were no back-bar mirrors and no bottles in sight. In short, this was a miners' saloon, ready for and always expecting trouble. He noted the presence of a cruising houseman, sawed-off pool cue tucked in his belt.

He found an empty space at the bar. There were five bartenders, all busy, but the closest one spotted him and presently came over. Will ordered, then remembered why he was here. He looked at the man on

28

his right, a sturdy, bearded, wool-hatted miner who smelled of sweat. How to begin, Will wondered. Not like politicians, by introducing himself. His whiskey came and he paid for it but did not drink it immediately.

He had to speak louder than usual to be heard in the din. He said, "I'm a stranger here. Why isn't everyone working?"

The miner shook his head and said something in a foreign language, then pushed away from the bar.

"You know damned well why they ain't." This came from his left, and Will turned his head to look at his neighbor. This was a big red-bearded man with bloodshot blue eyes and a whiskey-veined nose; his gravel voice was slurred with drink and was angry. He wore the rough working clothes of a miner.

"Yes, I guess I do. I was just making talk," Will admitted.

"You wouldn't be the Governor, would you?"

"No, I just work for him," Will said.

"I saw you in church," the miner said in a loud voice, as if accusing him.

"I was there, yes."

"And too damn proud to kneel or cross yourself," the man continued.

Will lifted his glass and drank, thinking, *Easy does it*. He wiped his mouth with the back of his hand, then looked at the miner. "It's not my church, friend. I don't know when to kneel or cross myself. Still, I was mourning like everyone else in your church."

"Mourning for pay," the miner said contemptuously. He raised an arm to signal the bartender and in doing so lurched into Will, who promptly moved to put more room between them.

"What caused the cave-in at the Mary E?" Will asked.

"Why, the goddamn owners," Redbeard said.

A voice behind Will said, "You'd better believe it." Will turned and confronted the houseman, a burly

29

young giant of a man with a broken, flattened nose that had never been set.

"You've both lost me," Will said. "How could the owners cause the cave-in?"

Redbeard said flatly, "They won't put in the timber they need. Miners come cheap. All you got to do after you kill 'em is pay for a pine box and a gravedigger. That's cheaper than timbering."

Will shifted his glance to the houseman. "You agree with that?"

"Hell, yes. I was a miner once. Look at my job. On this job I can get beat up or knifed or shot, but I can try and handle the trouble. There's no way you can handle a mountain caving in on you." He looked at Redbeard. "Sorry about Ed, Josh. A hell of a way to die."

"Ain't it?"

Will was looking closely at Josh. Tears were streaming from his eyes and disappearing into his beard, and now Will looked inquiringly at the houseman, who said, "Ed was Josh's brother. He was one of the twenty-one."

Before Will could even nod, he saw Phil Costigan move out from behind the houseman and confront him. Costigan had a fresh, unlit cigar wedged in the corner of his mouth; he hadn't shaved since Will saw him last, and his dirty grey turtleneck sweater held old food stains and was holed by burns from cigar ashes. He looked more like a saloon swamper than the literate, if prejudiced, editor that he was.

"Well, well," Costigan began. "How does it feel to be working for a jackleg lawyer?"

"I'm only on loan to him, and I like it," Will said.

"I didn't see you in church this morning."

"If they let you in any church, you were in the wrong one."

"Shake a lot of hands? Everyone promise to vote for Joe?"

The houseman looked at Will, "Who's he?"

"A non-friend of long standing," Will answered.

30

"Want him out?"

"Only if he wants to go out," Will answered.

The houseman then said to Costigan, "You want to go out?"

"What is this?" Costigan demanded hotly.

"A saloon," the houseman said. "What did you think it was?"

"I mean just what the hell are you trying to do? Muscle me out of here?"

"You're bothering a customer. I'm just paid to see you don't."

Costigan looked at Will. "Am I bothering you?"

"Yes, you've always bothered me," Will answered.

The houseman lifted a huge arm and pointed to the door. "The street's out there."

Costigan ignored him and surveyed Will with controlled anger. "You set up this hoorah?"

"No. Brady said you were in town and I hoped I wouldn't have to see you."

"Why are you here? Old Sam didn't send you. Joe did, didn't he?"

Will took a deep breath, "Yes, I work for him."

"What's his interest?" Costigan asked roughly.

"The working conditions at the Mary E. He's a state official with a right to ask questions and have them answered."

"The Mary E is one of the biggest mines in the state. What's the matter with it?"

Will nodded toward Josh, "Ask him."

Costigan looked at Josh. "All right. What's the matter with the Mary E?"

"The Mary E is a death trap; always was, always will be," Josh said flatly. "And they ought to hang Clay Hatcher from the headframe."

Costigan looked at him closely. "That's pretty strong talk, my friend."

"You ain't my friend, and the talk was meant to be stronger than that."

"You're drunk, old man," Costigan said contemptuously.

31

The houseman had heard enough. He reached behind Costigan, grasped his belt and the collar of his sweater, and lifted him off his feet. Turning, he toe-danced the helplessly struggling Costigan against the swinging doors, and when they opened he heaved him out into the street. Costigan sprawled into a passing miner and both men went down. The miner rose quickly, kicked Costigan in the head, brushed himself off and went on.

Will had followed the houseman to the swinging doors and now they stood together on the boardwalk, looking down at Costigan. The kick from the miner had dazed him. He looked up at them, recognition coming slowly, along with anger.

"I don't think he'll bother you any more," Will said.

"If he does, I'll do a better job on him."

Will said, "Thanks for handling him. I've wanted to do that for a long time."

He headed upstreet for the next saloon for more talks with miners. To a man, they told him the same story: not only was the Mary E unsafe, but most of the other mines were too. Only if they were working with a rich body of ore was there extensive timbering. Even then, it was less a safety measure than a guarantee they could tram out the rich ore. Winzes were seldom cut to ventilate the mines until the miners refused to work, or were unable to. There was no inspection of any sort except by the owners or the super.

Returning to his hotel, he found Cope talking with the middle-aged deputy sheriff who was seated beside him. Will shook hands with Sheriff Thompson, who soon excused himself and cruised upstreet. Will sat down in the chair the sheriff had vacated and was putting his hat on a neighboring chair when Cope asked, "What'd you find out, Will?"

Will told of his meeting with Costigan, and what had occurred inside the Bullseye and in front of it. Cope laughed soundlessly. Then Will gave him the gist of the miners' angry complaints and fears. Summing it up, he said, "They're absolutely helpless, Brady, and they

32

know it. I don't know how many men told me they were pulling up stakes. This cave-in scared them. Any one of them could have been among the twenty-one, and they know it." He paused. "Your turn."

Cope reflected for a few moments, then said wryly, "I've got the other side of it, naturally. Magruder said his miners are—and I quote—'dumb hunkies that don't speak or understand English and won't learn!' What he's saying is that his miners are uneducated, voteless and landless immigrants who aren't worth paying notice."

"How'd he explain away the cave-in?"

"He didn't try. He said, 'All mines everywhere are risky. We tell 'em that. Still, they want work and they get it.' "

"Get a look at the fourth level?"

Cope shook his head. "No chance. It's guarded. Too dangerous, Magruder said. I did find out one thing, though." He paused, isolating this. "Not all those twenty-one miners were crushed by falling rock. Ten of them close to the face were suffocated."

"No ventilation?"

Cope nodded. "They work the men in the tunnels until there is very little air. Only then do they cut a winze." He tapped the side pocket of his jacket. "I've got enough notes to fill a book, but who'll act on them?"

From across the tracks and in the yards came the clanking of railroad cars and the chuffing of engines. Cope rose tiredly, saying, "That's our train making up. Maybe we better get our stuff and mosey over there."

6

Belle was waiting on the depot platform for her father as the train pulled to a halt in the lowering dusk.

Cope stepped off ahead of Will, and Belle came out to meet them. She was dressed in a dark grey suit; she hugged her father, and as she did so her glance traveled appraisingly over Will's tall figure as he put down the luggage.

Cope turned, put an arm around Belle's waist and said, "Belle, you've never met Joe's secretary. This is Will Christie. Will, my daughter Belle."

Belle extended her hand, Will took it, and both murmured the amenities, Will with his hat in his hand.

Will looked from Belle to Cope. "Joe didn't tell me your family was here. I thought you lived up north near Meredith."

"We do. Belle decided she'd housekeep for me here, so I brought her down with me."

Will smiled. "At least you'll have a happy face to look at. There aren't very many of them around here."

Belle smiled too, pleased with this young man she had never heard of. She turned to her father then and said, "Pa, the hotel hack is waiting. Why don't we all three have supper together there? Then I'll tell you my surprise."

Cope was about to say something, thought better of it and smiled and nodded.

At the Granite Forks House, Will and Brady excused

themselves to wash off the train grime in Cope's room. As they came down into the lobby, Belle rose from her chair, and together, Brady in the middle, they moved through the wide dining-room doorway and were shown to a table by the buxom headwaitress. Both Brady and Will ordered a drink to be sent in from the bar just off the lobby and the waitress left them.

"Now, what's your surprise, Belle?"

Belle was about to speak, then looked closely at her father. "Damn it, Pa. You already know. I can tell."

"What do I already know?"

"That I've got us a house."

Cope pretended to be surprised. "Where?"

"The Hugh Evans place. You've been in it, Mrs. Evans said."

Cope nodded. "But where will Mrs. Evans live?"

"She's heading back for Illinois and her mother. There's nothing to keep her here except the house. I think she was even more glad to rent it than I was to get it."

The waitress came with their drinks, so Will could take his eyes off Belle. Both times on the train and in Twin Buttes he and Brady had talked nothing but politics and the Twin Buttes mining situation. Now, both of them lifted their glasses in silent salute to each other and drank.

Cope put down his glass and said, "I'm not sure I like this, Belle."

Belle asked plaintively, "Oh, Pa, why don't you?"

Cope thought a moment before answering. "Hugh Evans was a bad Attorney General. Old Sam's lackey. I said it on the Senate floor and I'll be saying it again."

Will said, "Maybe Mrs. Evans thought so too, even if she couldn't say it on the Senate floor."

Belle nodded. "Mrs. Evans likes you, Pa. She said I ought to be proud you're my father. If she really resented us would she have rented us her house?"

Cope looked from one to the other and said, "You two are teaming up on me." He shrugged. "I reckon if

I could live with Evans I can live with his ghost." He looked at Belle and smiled. "Let's take the house."

That settled, Belle was happy and showed it. Not so much to placate her father as to show she was truly interested in the errand he'd been on, the subject of conversation shifted immediately to the trip to Twin Buttes. Belle listened carefully, asking questions, commenting sometimes wryly, often with a deep sympathy for the miners. To Will, her thought processes reflected Brady's influence, but there was no doubt in his mind that she was her own girl.

When supper was finished it was still reasonably early and Will said he would excuse himself to drop by Joe's rooms. They were on the second floor of a pleasant frame house near the State House.

7

There were two men waiting in Cope's office when he walked in the next morning and he knew them both. One was a heavily bearded man in a townsman's suit named Miles Cheston, who was Hugh Evans' legislative assistant. The other was a ferret-faced, slim young man dressed in loafing clothes, who was Jimmy Day, Evans' secretary.

He shook hands with them, knowing what they wanted, and he thought each was entitled to some privacy in his interview, so he said, "Come into my office, Miles." He opened the door from the anteroom, which held three desks, two face-to-face, and one looking out into the corridor. Miles preceded him into the Attorney General's office, where there was a big desk, a high-backed leather-covered chair and two leather-covered easy chairs facing the desk.

Cope went behind the desk and sat down, and Miles, observing protocol, waited until he was seated before sitting down in one of the chairs facing the desk.

"Any plans, Miles?" Cope asked.

Cheston put both hands on his chair arms and rose.

"That answers the question I was going to ask, I reckon," Miles said.

"Yes," Cope agreed. "I want to pick my own staff, and you won't be on it."

Cheston nodded, pulled a keyring from his coat pocket and laid the keys on the desk.

"Thank you," Cope said. Cheston didn't offer to shake hands, nor did Cope. Cheston only nodded and walked to the door and let himself out.

Cope started around his desk, but halted abruptly. Something in this room was different from what it had been when he left, but what was it? Then he knew.

The locked filing cabinet which all visitors had to skirt on the way out of his office was no longer there.

He remembered, then reached in his right-hand jacket pocket and drew out a heavy envelope that bore the name Granite Forks House on the corner. He opened the envelope, shook out a set of keys and a note signed by Cato Jones. It was brief, informing Cope that he had cleaned out his desk and herewith returned the desk and door keys to the Attorney General's office.

Cope went to the door, opened it and saw Day sitting at his desk, while behind him Miles was cleaning out his belongings from his desk.

"Come in, Jimmy," Cope said. Jimmy rose and Cope stood aside to let him pass, noting the sulkiness in his alert and cynical young face.

Cope closed the door, saying, "Look around the room, Jimmy. Anything changed?"

Jimmy looked briefly, his glance halting at a spot by the door.

"Yes. What did you do with it?" Jimmy asked.

"When I left day before yesterday it was here. This morning it's gone," Cope said. "Do you know what was in it, Jimmy?"

"Not one single thing," Jimmy said flatly. "I could make a guess, but only a guess."

"Make it, then."

"Party stuff—'for your eyes only' letters, campaign collections. For sure, it was material he didn't want his staff to see."

Cope nodded, walked over to the desk, picked up Cato Jones's note, went over to Jimmy and handed it to him. Jimmy read it quickly. "Cato was here yesterday. Go find him, will you please?" Cope said.

"Am I working for you?" Jimmy asked.

"You are until you're told you're not."

Jimmy handed back Jones's note, turned and started out. He halted, turned to Cope and said, "What can Cato tell you that Miles and I can't?"

"We'll see," Cope said.

Jimmy shrugged and went out.

Cope spent the next hour going through the filing cabinets at the rear and at one side of Hugh Evans' desk. These were, in effect, summary files of the cases Hugh had handled during his years in office. They were purely reference files, Brady noted. The working files, of course, were behind Cheston's desk.

Brady had a file of folders spread on his desk when, an hour or so later, there was a sharp knock on his door. He called, "Come in," and Cato Jones stepped through the doorway, followed by Jimmy, who closed the door. Cato and Brady exchanged pleasant good mornings and Brady waved both men to chairs. The first thing Brady said was, "Thank you, Jimmy."

Brady seated himself, folded his arms and asked, "Jimmy tell you what this is all about, Cato?"

"He told me," Cato said grimly. He reached in his shirt pocket, brought out a piece of paper and held it out to Brady, who took it.

"While I was cleaning out my papers yesterday,

about ten o'clock I'd reckon, a couple of workmen showed up here and gave me this note from Mrs. Evans. They said they were here to pick up Hugh's locked file and take it to Mrs. Evans. Read the note, please."

Brady read it and looked up.

Cato continued. "Those were Hugh's personal files, or else they wouldn't have been locked. I told them to go ahead and take it and they did. Now, read what's written on the reverse side of the note, Mr. Cope."

Brady turned over the note and read aloud, " 'I did not send men to pick up Hugh's locked file. This note is an obvious forgery. This is my true handwriting; the writing on the reverse is not. Mrs. Hugh Evans. Witnessed by Jimmy Day and Cato Jones.' "

Brady looked up at Cato, who said, "Getting a sample of Mrs. Evans' handwriting was Jimmy's idea. When I showed him the note the men gave me he said we ought to check it with her. We went to her house and that's what she wrote." He wiped his sweating forehead with a pudgy hand. "I'm sorry, sir, I was—well, very skillfully deceived."

Brady read both sides of the note again, then asked Cato, "Was Mrs. Evans concerned about the loss of the file?"

Cato thought a moment. "I wouldn't judge so, sir. She was pretty mad that somebody had lied and used her name in a forgery. About the loss of the file she didn't express herself."

"Did you follow the men to make sure the file was loaded?"

Cato shook his head. "I'm afraid I didn't, sir. There wasn't any reason to."

"Of course not," Brady said. "In your place I'd have done just what you did." He rose. "Well, gentlemen, let's call it a day. Thank you all."

They rose, and Jimmy let Cato and Miles leave the office before he asked, "Am I still working for you, sir?"

Brady came around the desk, and he was already

moving his head in a sign of negation. He stopped in front of Jimmy and said, "No, Jimmy. I know where your loyalties are, and they're not with me, are they?"

"No, sir, I don't think they are."

Brady smiled. "With your reputation, Jimmy, you could walk into any office in this building and you'd be hired. Any office except Joe Isom's, that is."

Jimmy smiled. "No. I wouldn't even try that one."

"Tell Old Sam I said he's an idiot if he doesn't put you in his own office." He held out his hand, "Best of luck, Jimmy."

"Thanks, sir. My desk is cleaned out and my key is in the top right-hand drawer." He hesitated. "Best of luck to you, sir. I think you'll need it."

The door to Isom's anteroom was open, so that Will, hearing footsteps, looked up from his casebook and saw Brady enter. They exchanged good mornings and Cope said, "Can Joe see me, Will?"

Will rose, saying, "Go right in."

"You better come along too. It's something you'll want to know about." Puzzled by the gravity of Cope's voice and the hint of dying anger, Will tapped on the door to Joe's office, opened it and stepped aside for Brady.

Joe, at his desk, looked up, gave a loose wave of his hand toward the chairs and said, "Morning, Brady. You're my first caller since Old Sam got back. Sit down."

"I want Will to hear this too, Joe."

"Then both of you sit down."

When Will was seated Cope began with his discovery this morning that the file case was missing. Then he pushed Cato Jones's note across the desk to Joe, who read it and passed it to Will. Brady said that since obviously Cato had been in the office yesterday he had sent Jimmy Day to get him. As he gave the details of his interview with Cato he again reached in his pocket and produced the forged note, which both Joe and Will read, Joe without comment, Will with the observation: "Pretty damned coony."

"What do you think, Joe? Old Sam's orders?"

"I don't think he'd have done it this way, Brady. If he'd wanted the files he'd have asked the custodian to have them sent to his office. I doubt if he'd have dodged behind a forged note."

"Maybe our party boys, Brady?" Will asked.

"Possibly, but I don't think so," Cope said. "Even if they thought I'd object, certainly they would have told me first thing this morning. No, I doubt it, Will. I think someone knew those files held some big trouble for Old Sam. Whether they intend to use the files as blackmail against him, or just to protect Sam, I can't even guess."

The three men were silent for moments, puzzling this, and then Will spoke. "Want me to snoop around, Brady? I can say Joe is looking for some papers he can't find and thought they were in the files." Then Will shook his head, "Who would I be fooling?"

"Will, if Joe agrees, would you work on it?" He looked at Joe. "I'm short-handed, Joe. I fired the rest of Hugh's staff this morning."

"Will is still on loan to you, Brady." Joe smiled faintly. "Loan, I said. You can't keep him forever."

Now Brady spoke to Will. "You know any young fellows like you, Will? Any that would want to work for me?"

"Two or three. A fellow in the bank who's reading law; another at the feed stable."

"Send me the best first, Will."

"That'll be Jim Cousins. I'll see him," Will said.

8

From the front-page editorial of the GRANITE FORKS HERALD:

A PUZZLING PAIR OF BUZZARDS

Item: Hugh Evans, our state's Attorney General, died in his sleep last Sunday. (see column 3)

Item: Governor Kilgore was out of the state on a hunting trip when his long-time friend Evans died. Despite round-the-clock efforts of the Governor's staff to reach him with the sad news they were unable to get their message to him.

Item: Lieutenant Governor Joe Isom (Acting Governor in the absence from the state of Governor Kilgore) legally appointed a new Attorney General to succeed Evans *even before Evans was buried.*

Item: Three days after his appointment, Brady Cope, accompanied by Will Christie, the Lieutenant Governor's muscular so-called secretary, went down to Twin Buttes to view the mine disaster that took twenty-one lives. (see column 4) There, agitating among the miners, they tried to stir them up against the management of the Mary E Mine.

Item: On orders from Lieutenant Governor Joe Isom and carried out through Will Christie, your editor was injured and forcibly ejected from the Bullseye saloon in Twin Buttes while trying to obtain details of the mine disaster.

Questions:

1) Should our state tolerate a Lieutenant Governor who secretly and treacherously appointed an unqualified political crony to the office of Attorney General?

2) Should our state tolerate a man of proven incompetence as our Attorney General—a man whose first official act was to summarily dismiss the entire staff of the Attorney General's office?

3) As our headline stated, we have a peculiar pair of buzzards in the State House. How to get rid of them? Impeach them both.

Will Christie, seated at his desk in the anteroom, tossed the *Herald* on the desk, disbelief mingled with his mountain anger. Joe and Brady had been viciously libeled by Costigan's lies. Because Joe was half crippled and physically unable to thrash Costigan, and because Brady had a temperament that would reject the idea of using physical force, they would demand of Costigan a retraction and an apology, neither of which would be forthcoming.

He himself had been libeled in this scattering of lies, but there was something he could do about it that would avenge both Joe and Brady.

Leaving the copy of the *Herald* that he had bought from a newsboy in the corridor only moments ago, he picked up his hat, moved over to Joe's door, stuck his head in and said, "I'll be out for a while, Joe. I'll leave this door open so you can hear anybody coming in."

"All right," Joe said with no curiosity showing in his expression or in his tone of voice.

Will left the anteroom feeling only a little ashamed of himself for the sin of omission he was committing by not showing Joe Costigan's editorial. Still, Brady or someone else in the building would drop by to ask Joe if he had seen it. By that time, Will figured, there wouldn't be anything Joe could do about it.

At the foot of the Capitol steps he took a hack, asking the driver to stop at the *Herald* office. The ride had no soothing effect on him whatsoever; it only increased his impatience. When the hack pulled up in front of the dingy newspaper office, Will sat a moment longer staring through the open double doors. It wasn't too late to change his mind. Then he thought, *It has to happen sometime. Why not now?*

He told the hack driver to wait, then crossed the sidewalk and went past the double doors. There was a flat counter in front of him with a swing-gate separating it from the left wall. Beyond the counter was a big, paper-littered square desk. Past it was another swing-gate in the low railing that separated the office from the print shop. And in the print shop, Phil Costigan and his printer were working at the composing stone under a low-hanging shaded lamp.

The opening of the first swing-gate made a squeak that attracted Costigan's attention. The *Herald's* editor took only moments to identify Will, but in those seconds Will, not hurrying, had reached and passed the square desk and come to a halt in front of the second gate.

Costigan held a stick of type in his hand. He laid it on the stone, rubbed the palms of his hands down the bib of his inkstained apron, bent over, picked up a wooden mallet from under the stone, then straightened up and came over to the gate, facing Will.

"That didn't take long," Costigan observed. He reached under the bib of his apron, drew a cigar from his shirt pocket and put it in the corner of his mouth.

"Don't light it," Will said quietly. "It may wind up inside your belly."

Costigan pulled the gate open, gestured with a nod toward the chair across the desk from his own and said, "Sit down, Will, and get it off your chest."

He crossed in front of Will, tucked the mallet in his armpit, slapped his pants pockets for a match, then reached out to open the left-hand drawer. Remembering that Costigan was left-handed, Will put out both arms and lunged, shoving. Off balance now, Costigan crashed into the side wall and fell to his knees. The mallet dropped to the floor beside him. He picked it up, turned, plucked the mashed cigar from his mouth, threw it on the floor and lifted the mallet.

"You must want your face made over, Will," Costigan taunted.

Will took a step toward him, halted at the desk and pulled open the upper left-hand drawer. There, lying on a stack of copy paper, was Costigan's pistol. Will palmed it up, shifted it to his right hand, cocked it and said, "Throw that away—and not at me."

Costigan brandished the mallet and smiled. "That gun's empty. You think I'm crazy enough to load it?"

"Then it won't hurt if I pull the trigger."

He did. The gun blasted. Just to the side of Costigan's left cheek a hole appeared in the plaster wall. Save for the sifting down of plaster and the distant footfalls of the printer running for the alley, there were no other sounds.

Will had the reach, Costigan the weight. Only when Costigan wordlessly pitched the mallet over the counter. Will tossed his gun over the counter too. As if this were the signal, the two men charged each other. Costigan's nose was bleeding, his right eye beginning to close and his cut lip smarting did he realize that so far he had touched Will only on the forearms.

He came out of his crouch to gain some height and regretted it immediately. Will drove a fist into Costigan's solar plexus, driving the air from his lungs in an explosion of breath. He doubled over only to meet Will's knee coming into his face. In the fireworks of pinwheeling lights he wasn't aware of falling.

When his breathing became near normal, he opened his eyes. The ceiling was a dull view and he turned his head. When his eyes focused he could see Will Christie sitting on a corner of the desk, his left hand wrapped in a hankerchief, watching him.

Will rose now, came over and stood above him, seemingly half a mile tall.

"Can you hear me?"

Costigan spit out a mouthful of blood on his shirt

front, tried to talk and couldn't, then gave a painful nod that seemed to dislocate his neck.

Will said, "Don't bad-mouth Joe, me or Cope again, Phil. You do, and we'll have another waltz, like just now."

Phil said nothing, but he had heard. He drifted off to sleep or unconsciousness, but whichever, it felt good.

With the help of the hack driver, Costigan's printer got him in the hack. The printer knew where to direct the driver, and when they reached a mean, unpainted frame house with a now depleted vegetable patch for a front yard, the hack driver drove over it and pulled up at a side door. Together they carried Costigan into the long living room-bedroom and put him on the unmade bed. Besides the bed, the room contained only a small sofa, two straight-backed chairs, and a table against the front wall. The tiny room to the rear was the bathroom.

Costigan sighed deeply while the two men watched him, then he said through mashed lips, "Get the old lady next door."

The hack driver went out and waited while the printer went out to the front door, gave the message and then returned to the hack and drove off.

Some minutes later an old crone dressed in black came in without knocking. She looked at Costigan, then went into the bathroom, came out with a bowl and washcloth and, without speaking, began to clean up Costigan's bloody face. Costigan swore at her when she hurt him but she went stolidly on with her job. When she was finished she used her rudimentary English and said, "I bring supper."

9

Brady came out of the law library on the Capitol's third floor, and on the ground floor passed by his own locked door and entered the anteroom of Joe Isom's office. Will was not at his desk by the door, but Joe's office door was open. Joe must have heard him, for he called. "Come in."

Brady went into the big room where Joe, cane on his desktop, was reading a newspaper. They said hello and Joe waved him to a chair. Seated, Brady reached in his jacket pocket and as he drew out some notes he said, "I spent most of the afternoon upstairs in the law library, Joe. Found some interesting stuff."

"Talk to anybody up there?" Joe asked.

"Only the librarian. Why?"

"Then you haven't seen this?" Joe slid the newspaper across the desk and Brady leaned forward, picked it up, and the editorial in the black-bordered box caught his attention immediately. He read it through carefully, then drew a pencil from his jacket pocket and read it again, marking parts of it.

Afterwards his glance lifted to Joe and he said, "I think we can take care of this in court, Joe."

"I've got a feeling it's being taken care of already," Joe said. He went on to tell of Will's abrupt announcement that he was leaving the office for a while. Needing some correspondence that was in Will's files, Joe had passed Will's desk and seen the *Herald* on it and read the editorial.

At the finish of Joe's account Brady was smiling. "I wonder if he found a horsewhip?" he said.

"I don't think he'd need one," Joe said quietly. Then he added, "So you were in the law library?"

Brady put the paper aside and consulted his notes. While he was doing so he said, "I got curious about what we've got on the books on mine inspections. You're probably too young to remember the Somerset Mine fire."

"Only heard of it, Brady. What about it?"

"Well, it left fifty widows, and eighty men dead. The Somerset Mine District pushed for a bill that would have the Governor create the office of mine inspector. It required the office to inspect all mines, not only coal mines, once a year. If a mine had more than fifty men underground it was to be inspected every four months."

Joe frowned. "That law can't be on the books, Brady. I've never heard of it."

"Of course you haven't. There was such a reaction to the Somerset disaster that the legislature had to do something. They cooked up a bill creating the office of mine inspector and sat on it in conference until the clamor died down."

There came a growing noise out in the corridor of people walking and talking, and of doors closing and Brady realized that the workday was over. He rose, shut the door to the anteroom, came back and seated himself again. "Was the bill ever passed?" Joe asked.

"Yes. A watered-down version put the office—now hear this—under supervision of the Attorney General's office. It gave his office the right to set the amount of fines, subject to court approval."

"In other words, no fine if none is recommended by your office," Joe said. "Do I smell mine money behind it?"

"You do. With a compliant Attorney General in office it's no bill at all."

"Was a mine inspector ever appointed?" Joe asked.

"One," Brady answered. "I doubt if he ever inspected a single mine. In the next legislature the budget committee refused to approve the inspector's salary. It hasn't even been listed as a request in the last five budgets. As the Navy says of a destroyed ship, it was 'sunk without a trace.' "

Joe nodded. "Then the office is there, but pays no salary?"

"That's about it," Brady answered. "There were a couple of attempts to put the salary back in the budget, but they were defeated. Of the two men who sponsored the bill, one is dead and the other wasn't re-elected."

"What's your move, Brady?" Joe asked.

"I'll pay a mine inspector out of my own pocket," Brady said. "There'll be one, and he'll inspect."

There was a knock on the door and Will Christie stepped into the room. He said, "Hello, Brady," then his glance shifted to Joe. "Sorry I was gone so long, Joe. Anything for me?"

Joe regarded him carefully. "Have a nosebleed, Will?" he asked.

Will brought a hand up to his upper lip, looked at it and said, "No, why?"

"Then that's red ink on your shirt front?"

Will looked down, saw the spatter of bloodstains on his shirt and then sighed. "All right. It's from Costigan. We had a little disagreement."

"How little?" Joe asked.

"Well, let's say it was more than talk. He can't call me a 'so-called secretary' in that rag of his."

Brady was smiling. Joe and Will looked at each other and Joe said solemnly, "I agree with you, Will. That was uncalled-for."

"A gratuitous insult," Brady said.

All three exchanged sober glances. Joe Isom was the first to break into laughter, followed by Brady and Will.

"It must have been fun," Joe said. "Tell us about it."

Will skirted Brady's chair, sat down on its twin and

told what had happened; since he had not mentioned Joe or Brady in his conversation with Costigan he was free to tell the whole truth.

When he was finished, Brady observed, "That's quicker than the courts, Joe. Still, I miss the horse-whip."

"Next time," Will promised. "I was in a hurry."

All three men knew Will's true reason for thrashing Costigan, but it was never to be brought up in the future.

Brady said, "I was telling Joe what I found in the law library this afternoon." He went on to tell Will of his findings and of his intent of appointing a mine inspector.

When he was finished Joe said, "Who've you got in mind for the job, Brady?"

"I haven't thought about it, Joe, except I think I might be able to get a good man on loan from one of the mines that really practice safety inspection. And, speaking of loans, you said you'd loan me Will to track down my missing files. Will you loan him to side my mine inspector?"

"Certainly," Joe said. "But I don't think Will knows his way around a mine. Do you, Will?" When Will shook his head Joe gave Brady an inquiring look.

"I think we might work it this way, Joe," Brady said. "I'll give my mine inspector a 'To Whom It May Concern' letter confirming his appointment and quoting his statutory authority to inspect any mine. You give Will a similar letter asking all mines to cooperate with the state mine inspector."

"You're expecting trouble," Will said.

"Of course. If my inspector goes in alone to a mine company they'll laugh at him and tell him to get off their property. But if he goes in with Will and has a letter from the Lieutenant Governor, they'll take some notice. I can appoint Will a deputy marshal. That'll give him not only the power of arrest, but the authority to issue a court summons. Mining companies may laugh at my mine inspector but not at Will's authority."

"So they submit to inspection or are taken to court," Joe said.

At Brady's nod, Joe said, "Will, how's it sound?"

"Anything that gets me out of the State House sounds fine," Will said. "How do we travel?"

"How do you want to travel?" Brady asked.

"By horse with a pack horse," Will replied. "That is, if it's agreeable with your inspector."

"I'll make that a condition, and it makes sense. I'll want him to hit the mines away from the railroads and the telegraph first. Once you hit the big mines on the railroad the telegraph wires will be burning up. I'd like you to have a backlog from mines already inspected before you hit the big boys."

"Anything Old Sam can do to you, Brady? If there is, he'll do it."

"The law is on the books. Let him try."

10

When Costigan awakened in the morning and got his bearings, he swung his feet over the side of the bed and put his foot in his supper which had been placed on the floor beside the bed.

He rose, lurched to the table, groaning with pain. From the single drawer he took out a cigar, lit it and went back to bed. He lay there trying to recall and assess what had happened to him yesterday at the *Herald*. The shame of his beating at Christie's hands stoked an anger and impotent fury in him. Hurting as he was, he could only think of revenge on Christie. He knew that any future attack on Isom or Christie would only bring a repeat of what had happened yesterday. Christie had told him so.

His thoughts became confused and contradictory, and he had sense enough to know that his brain was still addled from the beating he had taken. He threw his half-smoked cigar into the plate of food, then lay back and went to sleep.

He was aroused at mid-morning by a knock on the door. To hell with answering it, Costigan thought. Whoever it was would go away.

The knock came again and a voice called, "Let me in, Phil."

It was Frank Jackson's voice. Costigan rose, crossed to the door and opened it.

The two men regarded each other in a moment of silence, then Jackson said softly, "Good God, man! You look as if one of our trains ran over you."

"That's how I feel, too. Come in, Frank."

The older man stepped in, took off his hat and removed a cigar box from under his arm and held it out, saying, "The way you look I don't know if you can handle these."

They were fine cigars, and Costigan thanked him. He gestured toward a chair and went back to the bed and sat down on it. "The word's out, I take it."

Jackson nodded. "The hack driver took care of that. Tell me about it, but not before I have a chance to say your editorial was damned good. Fair and accurate."

Costigan nodded his thanks. "If I could have got to my gun in the desk drawer I could have handled him, but he beat me to it." He went on to describe the fight, leaving out nothing. He finished by saying, "I just couldn't get to him, Frank."

"Will you write it up, just like it happened?"

Costigan shook his head. "No. He said if I bad-mouthed him, Cope or Joe again he'd be back. I believe him, and once is enough," Phil said gloomily.

"Then you'll let it slide?"

"No. I'd like to have him get just what he gave me.

I really haven't thought it through, Frank."

"What have you figured so far?"

Scowling, Costigan picked up the new box of cigars and pried open the lid. There on top of the cigars was a big package of bills. Costigan looked inquiringly at Frank, who said, "For your editorial, with our thanks."

Costigan thanked him again, pocketed the bills, then offered him a cigar, which Jackson politely declined. Costigan fired one up and appreciated the flavor for a moment.

"You were about to say how far you'd figured," Jackson prompted.

"I want Joe beat up," Costigan said flatly.

"You can't. He's a cripple now. You'll kill him."

"What about Christie? Joe'll get the message. He sends a man to beat me up, I can send someone to beat up his man."

Frank rose and took a turn around the room, hands in hip pockets. Finally he said, "I like the idea, but it's risky. If our men are caught—and there's always that chance—they'll say they were paid by an unknown party. That'll point straight to you." Suddenly he halted, pulled a hand out of his pocket and snapped his fingers. "I've got it!"

He walked over and faced Costigan. "It's staring us in the face. Go back in your *Herald* files. Read about the trial of that rustling ring that made Isom famous. Those the ranchers didn't hang on the spot got long prison sentences, didn't they?"

Costigan nodded, saying, "And they're still in prison, so that's out."

"Is it? Most of those rustlers had brothers, fathers, uncles and cousins and nephews. We pick from that bunch. If they're caught and say they were paid by an unknown party, who'll believe them? They were out to get even with Will Christie and Joe Isom for testifying against their relatives and jailing them. Revenge, Phil. Who'll think of you when better motives for beating Christie are plain? Not Isom."

"He'll think of it."

"But will he act on it? I doubt it, and that's all you're concerned with."

Phil thought this over. It was a good idea but impossible to carry out, and he voiced his reasons for thinking so. "Hell, Frank. Those kinfolk are scattered over the state and the territories. I don't have the time or money to dig 'em out."

"We're a railroad. We have passes on other railroads and feeder stagelines. On that pass a man can travel anywhere in the West."

"But I got a paper to put out if I want to eat."

"You get the names and where they live off the trial records at the State House. Leave the rest to me and the man I'll send out to hunt these people down. He'll be a good man, one of ours."

Phil was thoughtful for a full minute and Jackson waited patiently. When Costigan spoke he said, "Frank, I don't want Christie killed. How do I know he won't be?"

Jackson smiled. "Easy. Half down payment to whoever is hired, half afterwards. We tell him if Christie is killed, we give the name of the killer to the closest U. S. marshal. What else?"

"Nothing, I guess."

11

Belle was sitting on the top step of her porch, saddlebag by her side, when Will rode up to the tie rail leading a small grey saddled mare. It was a cloudless fall morning with no wind, and as she walked out of the gate in her brown divided skirt and matching jacket she said, "Somebody up there must have been saving this day for us, Will."

"That's what I ordered yesterday," Will answered. "I've shortened the stirrups. Try 'em."

Belle swung up, settled herself in the saddle and said, "Just right."

Together they rode down the street, turned left on Front Street and headed for the Sisters shouldering up to the west.

"Tell me about this Jim Cousins, Will. Do you think Pa'll scare him?"

"Your father doesn't scare people like Jim. He'll like him and so will you." He thought a moment, then added, "I don't know much about him except he's another one of us that wants to be a lawyer. He worked for the feed stable until last week. He quit to help his father build a line shack. I think they're a big family, and Jim's the oldest. Hugh Evans wanted to take him on, but his father had quarreled with Old Sam and that ended it."

Past the edge of town they picked up an old weed-grown logging road long since abandoned, although the course of it was easily picked out because the trees had been logged out.

Will noticed that Belle was as at home astride a horse as he was. As he rode into the morning he questioned her about the ranch up north close to Meredith. It turned out they had a small ranch, employing only three hands, and Brady rode to his office in town each day no matter what the weather was. Belle told him she had grown up mostly with boys, and by the time she had finished schooling there she was such a roughneck that her parents had become alarmed. They had shipped her off to a girls' school in St. Louis to have some of the rough edges taken off. Will grinned when she told him that it had taken a year before she learned to carry on an ordinary conversation without swearing.

Their ride through the early morning was through big ponderosas that had been logged out on both sides of the trail. As they got into higher country they thinned out and gave way to occasional meadows of wild hay through which small alder-hooded creeks flowed.

By mid-morning the rutted old road snaked out of the timber and headed across a big valley bisected by a stream whose banks were lined with dense choke-cherry bushes.

On either bank of the stream there was a sloping dugway whose grade was gradual enough to accommodate big timber wagons. Will reined aside to let Belle's grey mare precede him down the dugway and into the stream. Belle's mare had almost reached the creek when she suddenly spooked and reared almost upright. Belle, caught by surprise, slid out of the saddle and over the mare's rump, dropping to the ground on the dugway.

Will looked upstream and saw a big cinnamon bear with a cub on either side of her, standing in the water against the far bank, feeding off berries. The bear had wheeled when the grey reared and now growled and began its clumsy charge.

Belle came to her feet quickly and Will put his horse to the left, roweled him and came up on Belle's left, leaning out of the saddle. He wrapped his arm across her back and under her right arm, lifted, and put his horse across the stream and up the opposite dugway. The bear altered course, growling savagely, and took off after Will's horse.

As soon as the horse had taken the grade of the dugway and was on flat ground it was no sort of race, the horse easily leaving the bear behind. Now that the danger was over, the bear turned back down the dugway to her cubs and Will reined in. He gently set Belle's feet on the grass.

He looked down at her and saw the excitement still bright in her eyes. "The old girl had two males to pick on, but what did she do? Charge the females. Are you all right?"

"Yes. I landed where I have the most padding."

Will looked back and saw that the bear had vanished, then he rode over to Belle's mare, caught the reins and led her back to Belle. She mounted, but then sat still in the saddle.

"I was waiting for your shot when you picked me up. I'm glad you didn't shoot her, Will."

"No. Somebody had to tell those cubs that they just saw an honest-to-god girl."

"A scared one," Belle said quietly. "Thanks, Will. I have the feeling you've done that before."

"No, but I've been in plenty of chicken pulls. That's even harder."

"What's a chicken pull?"

Will explained then that on the big ranch he grew up on where his father was foreman, they had Sunday horse races and chicken pulls. For the chicken pull, a chicken was buried so that only its head and neck were above ground. The rider, whose horse was at a dead run, had to lean out of the saddle, reach down and seize the chicken around the neck. Any miscalculation would result in either no chicken or a sprawling spill out of the saddle.

"Where was the ranch, Will?" Bell asked.

"In New Mexico," Will said. He went on to describe the big Spanish land grant, long held by the same Spanish-American family. All the children of the men and women who worked on the ranch were made to go to the ranch's own school, where a hired tutor and his wife were the teachers. As he looked back on it, Will said, it was the best possible kind of school and the best way of life. The *patrón* was both generous and protective. When Will had become of an age where he wanted to strike out on his own, he was rated a top hand. He worked for several big outfits, hunted wild horses for a time, then took the job of brand inspector. It was during this time that he had met Joe Isom. In answer to Belle's gentle questioning he said that he could only barely remember his mother and his father, who had died of smallpox on a cattle-buying trip to Mexico.

As Jim Cousins had told Will, if they stuck to the old logging road they couldn't miss the line camp where he and his father were working. Toward midday they came to the cabin of freshly peeled logs that Jim and his father were building. They had spotted it on the far edge of a clearing, and its freshly peeled logs gleamed pinkly in the sunshine. Its roof of sod on poles blended into the background of ponderosas, and Will knew that once the logs had weathered he would almost have to stumble on the shack before he could see it.

Jim, working at the stream mixing mud for chinking, saw them first. He dropped his hoe, washed his hands and came toward them. He was a wiry young man, middle-sized, and when he took off his hat to meet Belle she could see his smiling mouth. As he came over to meet them, an older man, bucksaw in hand, came out of the shack and saw them, leaned the saw against the wall and came over to where Belle and Will had dismounted.

The older man was slight and small-boned, with a fierce-looking grey mustache that was belied by his mild blue eyes. Belle shook hands with both Jim and his father, and afterwards the four of them moved out of the sunshine into the shade of the big pines. Will and Jim brought saw logs from the big woodpile for them to sit on.

Will led the horses into deep shade and brought the saddlebags back with him, and when he came back Jim was saying, "The heavy work is done and Dad can finish the rest."

Jim looked at Will then and said, "Miss Belle just said her father would like me to come down as soon as I can. Think tomorrow will be soon enough?"

Will nodded and took a deep beath of the pine-scented air that was wafting over from the pile of green bark that had been peeled from the logs.

When Belle asked to see the cabin, Mr. Cousins showed her inside. Jim asked Will questions about what his new job would call for, but Will was purposefully vague. He thought Brady deserved a chance to explain Jim's job to him, rather than having Jim rely on possible misinformation from Will.

Afterwards, when Belle and Jim's father came outside, Belle opened the saddlebag from her horse. She had cooked enough chicken last night for the four of them, and they had a pleasant meal in the shade of the big trees. During the meal Belle told Mr. Cousins of their encounter with the bear and her cubs. All the men agreed that a detour around the park was called for on the return trip.

Will and Belle took their leave soon afterwards. Jim and his father watched them until they were out of sight.

Presently Jim's father said, "This what you been waiting for?"

"Yes, Pa. Even better. He's the best lawyer in the state. If I can't learn from him, I can't learn from anybody."

"Well, inside work don't hurt a man, I reckon. Me, I never tried it."

Jim looked at his father, smiled and said, "Neither have I, but I'm about to."

12

Three days later Will and the state's new mine inspector reined in their hard-breathing horses on the crest of a bare butte at the base of which lay scattered frame buildings and the headframe of the Calcutta Gold Mine, along with a water tank, windmill and dormitories.

"Your memory's pretty good, Kevin," Will said to Kevin Lloyd, now on loan to the Attorney General by the big Veteran Gold Mines. He was a sturdy Welshman of middle age with a pepper-and-salt beard that matched a bear-trap jaw beneath the darkest of brown eyes. Like Will, he was dressed in rough worn range clothes. In his saddle scabbard, instead of a carbine, was a tight roll of maps.

"That water tank looks mighty good," Kevin said in a gravelly voice.

They split up to find a trail down the butte's sloping face; Will found one first and hallooed Kevin over. On the flats below they headed for the windmill beside the tank and big adobe corral. There they let their three horses drink, and took turns themselves drinking and soaking their heads in the stream of fresh water from the windmill's pipe. Afterwards both men dried their hair and faces with their neckerchiefs and looked around at the weather-scoured frame buildings.

There was some shade cast from the noisy blacksmith shop and they led their horses over to it and tethered them. Then Kevin said. "See that fellow standing in the door of the shack past the dormitory. That's Shroeder, the owner."

"All right," Will said, starting toward the building.

"Let me tackle the old bastard first," Kevin said.

As they approached, Shroeder put the point of his heavy shoulder against the doorframe, crossed his booted feet at the ankles and regarded them in surly disapproval. He was a big-bellied man, meaty-faced and bald, with a fringe of grey hair over his ears.

"If you're ridin' the chuck line, stay the night and then keep ridin'," Shroeder said. "Our grub is shy and we need it."

"You don't remember me, do you, Shroeder?" Kevin said.

The heavier man looked at him closely. "No, should I?"

"Kevin Lloyd. I was your shift boss once."

"I remember. The beard had me fooled." Neither

man offered to shake hands, Will observed. "What is it you want, Lloyd? If it's a job, look somewhere else."

"No. I want to inspect your mine."

"What for? It's not for sale."

Kevin walked over to him, took out the "To Whom It May Concern" letter that Brady Cope had provided him with, and extended it. Shroeder opened the envelope, read the letter, then looked at Kevin. "Mine inspector. What the hell is this? There ain't no mine inspector. And who's this Brady Cope that calls himself Attorney General? Hugh Evans is Attorney General." He tossed the letter contemptuously at Kevin's feet.

Kevin ignored it, but lifted his thumb over his shoulder. "Meet Will Christie. He's deputy state marshal. He'll tell you some things."

Shroeder uncrossed his ankles and straightened up.

Will moved past Kevin and extended his hand, saying, "Howdy, Mr. Shroeder."

Shroeder wiped his hand on the seam of his trousers before shaking hands. He was, Will guessed, both awed and puzzled that a marshal was Kevin Lloyd's companion.

"What's all this about mine inspection?" Shroeder asked in a still belligerent tone of voice.

"You just read the letter Kevin gave you. I've got another one." Will reached in his hip pocked and pulled out a saddle-flattened envelope, opened it and handed it to Shroeder, saying, "Here's a copy of the statute creating the office of mine inspector. It's still on the books."

Shroeder read it, his frown deepening. Finished, he slapped the letter with his free hand. "Like Kevin's, this here is signed by Brady Cope, Attorney General. He ain't. Hugh Evans is, because I know him."

"Evans died ten days ago. Cope was appointed in his place," Will said quietly. "I reckon the news just hasn't reached you."

Shroeder scowled. "You're damned right it hasn't."

61

He looked from Will to Kevin. "What do you want to inspect in my Calcutta?"

"For safety, mainly. You heard about the cave-in at the Mary E, didn't you?"

"I heard," Shroeder said grimly. "What's that got to do with my mine?"

"Well, if they'd timbered a couple of places in Number Four level that never would have happened," Kevin said.

"I don't recollect there's any timber close to the Mary E. Like here. You see any close?"

Kevin lifted a thick arm and pointed to a range of mountains which, at this distance, looked black compared to the desert floor.

"The Palmers?" Shroeder ask incredulously. "Hell, they're fifteen, twenty miles off."

"Any miner that can single-jack can swing an axe. You freight your ore to steel so you get the teams and wagons. If you can't spare your miners to cut timber, then buy it and freight it from steel. If you need it, that is."

"Timbering costs money, a hell of a lot," Shroeder said vehemently.

"If you're in good ore it's a damn sight cheaper than cleaning out a cave-in that you'll have to timber afterwards." When Shroeder held a sullen silence Kevin asked, "You working any Cousin Jacks, Shroeder?"

Cousin Jacks were Welshmen, trained in the mines of Cornwall, and were exceptionally skilled in timbering. Shroeder knew this and now he pounced. "Oh, no you don't, Lloyd. I give you one of them to show you the mine, he'll say everything underground needs timbering."

"I'll be the judge of that," Kevin said. "I was thinking a smart Cousin Jack with a tape and a notebook could be a help to us both. I point out what needs timbering. He measures roof or walls, or both. When we're done you'll know how much timbering you'll need and what it'll cost in timber and work time. You'll get a hundred and twenty days to complete it."

62

While Kevin talked Shroeder's face had grown darker. When he finished, Shroeder took a step backwards, reached to the side of the doorway and brought up a shotgun which he held by the barrel with his huge fist.

Taking a step forward, he said, "Now get this, both of you. You're on private property. You weren't invited on it, so get the hell off it, and quick!" He raised the gun waist high.

"You're in real trouble right now, Shroeder," Will said quietly. He looked at Kevin. "Go get my rope, Kevin."

Kevin turned and started for the horses.

"Go along with him and don't come back!" Shroeder snarled.

"No," Will said. "Point that gun at me and you're under arrest."

"Damned if I need it!" Shroeder shouted. He threw the gun from him and charged at Will, both arms drawn back, fists clenched, bellowing like a bull. Will stepped aside and tripped him. Shroeder hit the ground and, cat-quick, rolled on his side, pushed himself erect and spread his arms, welcoming Will's rush, and moved to meet it.

Will drove a fist in Shroeder's fat belly. It was like hitting a sack of packed sand. Shroeder's arms embraced him in a massive bear hug.

Will knew he was fighting a true barroom brawler who would break his back if he could. He shifted tactics. As Shroeder locked his hands behind Will's back, Will lifted his knee into Shroeder's groin and as his leg descended his bootheel smashed into Shroeder's instep. This had a triple effect; Shroeder dropped his hands to protect his groin, bent over in pain, put his weight on the foot Will had just stomped, and when it gave way under him fell ponderously on his side. Will kicked him in the jaw and Shroeder simply rolled over on his back, arms loose, eyes unseeing.

Will stood astride his heavy body, waiting for Kevin.

When he came they rolled Shroeder over on his belly, tied his hands behind his back with Will's rope, ran the rope to his ankles and tied them together. Will then rolled Shroeder on his back.

When he began to stir Will stepped astride him and sat down on his big belly.

"Shroeder. I'm talking to you. Can you hear me?"

"Get off me," Shroeder grunted.

"Not yet. I've got something to tell you. Since you attacked a deputy marshal you're under arrest. I'm taking you back to Granite Forks—but not yet, Shroeder. I'm going to tie you on your horse and you'll come with me. We may be gone two weeks before we reach the Forks. How does that sound, Shroeder?"

The only part of his body Shroeder could move was his head and now he rolled it from side to side. "You can't do that!" he shouted. "I got to be here. My miners will steal me blind and wreck my machinery."

Will nodded. "Sure they will. Still, there's a way out of it for you, Shroeder."

Shroeder was silent and he watched Will balefully. Finally he said, "What way?"

"Why, give us permission to inspect your mine, you damned fool."

"Then you won't take me?"

"That's right."

"Then get off me and untie me," Shroeder growled.

"I haven't heard you give permission," Will said stubbornly.

"All right. Inspect it!" Shroeder shouted.

Will rose, and he and Kevin rolled Shroeder over on his face and untied his bonds, then stepped back. Shroeder came to his feet, dusted off his clothes and muttered, "Come on."

Shroeder went inside the office, returned with a map and headed for the hoist shack. Kevin followed him. Will watched them go, and he wondered if they could expect this same routine at each mine they were to inspect. *Very probably,* he thought.

13

That same afternoon Brady Cope's new secretary, Jim Cousins, entered Brady's office with some papers in hand, laid them on the desk, and said, "Will that be all, Mr. Cope?"

Brady looked up from a file folder whose contents he had been leafing through, leaned back in his chair and said, "Yes. We're done for the day, Jim."

He looked at the wiry young man standing before him, the man whose name he had got from Will. Along with many other young men here, Cousins wanted to pick up experience in law at a Capitol office but had found all the jobs filled with relatives of Old Sam's awesome machine. Then Will had located him up in the Sisters Range working for his father.

Brady asked, "After two days, how're you liking it?"

"I like it now, sir, and I'll like it better."

"Good. See you tomorrow, Jim."

When Cousins was gone Brady looked at his watch and realized it was time for him to be tired and hungry, and he was both. Taking two of the file folders, he left. Locking the anteroom door, he went outside and saw the hack stand area was empty. He hated the walk down the hill but there was nothing else for it, so he took the gravel drive and headed down the shaded street his house was on.

The Evans house had been freshly painted this summer, he judged. It was a grey color with smart white trim, a two-story building with just enough side yard to give it more privacy than its neighbors.

He went through the gate of the white picket fence, climbed the porch steps and went inside. Belle was in the kitchen, heard the door close and called, "You're working late, Pa." Brady crossed the carpeted living room, went through the dining room and halted in the kitchen doorway.

"Something smells good, but don't tell me what it is. I want to be surprised."

Belle, at the sink, turned, smiled and said, "I won't. You want me to mix you a drink, Pa?"

Brady nodded. "A dark one. Let me put this stuff away." He opened on his left a door and walked into Hugh Evans' library, a small book-lined room where there was an easy chair, an open roll-top desk and a swivel chair. Beyond the desk was another easy chair, and beside it a table holding a shaded reading lamp.

Brady started to shrug out of his coat and head through the space between the chair and the roll-top desk, which was stuffed to capacity with papers, files and account books. As Brady passed it, the skirt of his coat dragged across the front of the desk and, as if it had hit the key paper of this paper jam, the entire contents of the desk cascaded against him and onto the floor.

Brady tossed his files onto the seat of the easy chair and took off his coat, swearing all the while. He pitched his coat on the chair's back, circled around the swivel chair and walked out the way he had entered and went into the kitchen.

He came up beside Belle, who was making his drink, and said, "Belle, what the devil are all those papers jammed in the library desk? What are we supposed to do with them?"

"Pa, I told you, Mrs. Evans cleaned out her safe-deposit box the afternoon she left. She was in a tizzy to finish packing and catch the train. She told me to hold them until Cato Jones picked them up. He's her new lawyer."

Brady grumbled, "If I know Mrs. Evans—and I do —she probably forgot to tell him the stuff was here."

Belle put down Brady's drink in front of him, saying, "Well, just shove them back in the desk and pull down the roll-top."

"I've already shoved them the wrong way," Brady said. "They're on the floor."

"Leave them. I'll pick them up later."

"No, I'll put them back." Picking up his drink and looking at the color, he said, "This'll give me the strength of ten."

He walked back into the library, surveyed the pile of papers, took a deep drink from his glass and set the glass on the desktop. Afterwards he got down on his knees and began picking up the papers. He paid no attention to them, stuffing them tightly into the back of the desk, until after he had deposited the third bundle. He looked down at the pile and saw, face up, a scattering of what were unmistakably stock certificates. He could not help but see in big red block letters the legend, The Mary E Mine, Inc. He had heard that Hugh Evans was a stockholder in the Mary E, but he resisted the temptation to count the number of shares.

Some of the certificates had fallen face down, and as he picked these up his glance fell to the two names boldly inscribed in ink. The bottom signature was Hugh Evans; the top signature, in Evans' handwriting, was that of Samuel Kilgore.

Brady picked up one of the certificates and saw that what Hugh Evans had signed was a transfer of certificate of stock to Sam Kilgore.

Brady put down the certificate, turned over those he already held in his hand and leafed through them all. All told the same signed story.

Still on his knees, Brady came to a conclusion he could hardly believe. He rose, reached for his glass, took a long drink and thought, *Clay Hatcher's bribe to Old Sam. The best way he could do it was to issue stock to Hugh Evans. Hugh would vote the stock. The dividends would be paid to him, and he'd pay Old Sam and call it a political contribution. But the stock value is Old Sam's.*

He heard Belle's voice then, "Supper's almost ready, Pa."

14

Governor Sam Kilgore caught it first.

He and Frank Jackson had spent the day hunting turkeys up in the Seven Sisters west of town, and just before dark they rode out of the thick piñons into an open wild-hay meadow. At its far edge was what Jackson referred to as his line camp. It consisted of two large log buildings separated by a bridged creek, and as they rode closer they could see lamps were lighted in both buildings.

Two of Frank's crew had been sent ahead with the birds and guns. As they approached the corral one of the crew took the horses and they headed afoot for the bridge. As they passed the bunkhouse, he noticed a horse at the wooden tie rail by the bunkhouse. Frank made a small detour to read the brand in the half-light, saw it was his own and joined Old Sam at the bridge. Sam led the way up and had his foot on the porch steps when he saw a man rise out of the porch chair.

From behind Old Sam Frank said, "What are you doing here, Bobby?"

"Telegrams for the Governor, Frank. Here you are, Governor."

Bobby was the oldest hand Frank employed at his F Lazy J ranch below. Old Sam said hello and thanks almost in the same breath.

"Did you have a drink, Bobby?" Frank asked.

"Sure. I lit the lamps. I figured it was owing."

"If you weren't so damned old, I'd fire you," Frank said. "Come on in."

Old Sam had crossed the pleasant carpeted room whose walls of square-cut logs had been whitewashed. He chose an easy chair by the brightest lamp and slacked into it. Frank went over to a far corner where there was a table set for two, moved behind it to a temporary bar on the sideboard and began to pour drinks. Bobby, hat off, sat in a chair nearest the door.

For minutes the only sounds in the house were the rustle of paper from Old Sam's telegrams and the cook moving around in the kitchen.

Frank came over, put Old Sam's drink on the table holding the lamp and then moved to the easy chair on the far side of the lamp. Old Sam finished, picked up his drink and handed the telegrams to Frank across the table.

"Any answer?" Frank asked. When Old Sam shook his head, Frank said, "Go get your supper, Bobby. We may have something in the morning."

Bobby said good night and went out, and now Frank put his attention to Old Sam's telegrams. He read them through and saw they were much alike. They were all from big mining companies. A two-page one from Magruder, the superintendent of the Mary E, said Christie and Lloyd had telegraphed him they would be in Twin Buttes on October 15th to inspect the Mary E. He demanded to know by what authority the Lieutenant Governor's marshal and a mine inspector appointed by the Attorney General's office had the right to inspect his mine, and questioned the legality of the authorization.

As a reminder to Old Sam he listed the taxes present and past paid to the state by his mines. This was pure harassment of an honorable corporation which had long supported the Governor. There was more, including threats of court action. Amazingly (*and very indiscreet*, Frank thought), Amalgamated's telegram said that in the past ten years they had contributed heavily to the party, and had paid generously to avoid confrontations such as this, and they expected the protection they had bought. The other two telegrams, one from High Country Minerals and the other from the Happy Jack, both registered vigorous protests and asked for information.

Frank put the telegrams on the table and said, "That probably explains Christie's disappearance this past week."

Old Sam took a pull on his drink, wiped his mustache with the back of his fist and said, "I thought that damned bill was dead for good. Where's Cope getting the money to pay his inspector?"

"He's not a poor man," Frank said.

"Is it legal for him to pay the inspector?"

Frank smiled. "Ask your Attorney General."

Old Sam smiled too at Frank's answer, but not with any enjoyment. He looked at him and said, "They've got me over a barrel, Frank."

Frank sipped on his drink and said, "I don't see it that way." Old Sam waited, watching Frank, who was frowning in thought. Then Frank said, "All right. The legislature's in session. Hanson is the minority leader in the House. Suppose he takes the floor to protest the unfairness of the present bill?"

"Unfairness—how?"

Frank went on, "With a single mine inspector, it'll take two or three years to inspect all the mines. What about those already inspected? They'll be forced to spend money to meet the safety standards, while the majority of mines go scot free of them for a couple of years. What's fair about that?"

"But the damned law is on the books, Frank."

"But it doesn't have to stay. Say Hanson introduces a bill creating a ten-man Mining Commission to be appointed by the Governor. The commission will have the power to hire a dozen or fifteen mine inspectors to get the job done quickly."

Now Old Sam's smile was genuine. "I get it," he

said. "I back Hanson's bill. I promise to appoint five members of each party to the commission."

Frank nodded. "Since the opposition party introduced the bill, you want to be absolutely fair in your commission appointments."

"Will Hanson go along with this?" Old Sam asked.

"Why wouldn't he? It makes him a white knight, and also a little richer from the money we give him."

"I break a tie vote if the commission's split, don't I?"

Jackson made an impatient gesture with his hand. "You'll never have to vote, Sam. From the first meeting it'll be a dogfight. From the beginning there'll be a row over hiring inspectors. Charges and countercharges, pleas for injunctions, court fights for years, suits brought by the mining companies charging discrimination and prejudicial inspections."

Now Frank leaned forward, elbows on knees, and looked at the Governor. "You see, Sam, the men you appoint to the commission won't want safety inspections. All they'll want, both parties, is Cope out of inspection authority. This bill will take the authority away from him."

"That'll work, Frank. It's good. It's so good it prompts me to ask you a question." He paused. "Would you take on Hugh's old job—state party chairman?"

Frank frowned and was silent a moment. "Would that be wise, Sam? I'm a railroad man, and we're not loved by everybody."

"You don't have to be loved. Our party bylaws say the chairman is responsible for raising and disbursing campaign funds. Hell, Hank Davidson is his party's chairman. He owns half a dozen big ranches."

Frank nodded. "A money raiser. Yes, I can do that. But I'll have to consult with our directors first."

Sam nodded. "You might tell them that you are necessary to the party. And right now you won't be bragging, because it's true."

71

15

Kevin and Will hit Twin Buttes' Main Street in early afternoon. Their first stop was the feed stable fronting the tracks. Their horses were tired, and they both were hungry and dusty, but as soon as they had caught sight of Twin Buttes an hour before, they had agreed to hit the Mary E first thing when they got to town. The thought of the Mary E had been teasing them for days and they both wanted it out of the way as quickly as possible.

Side by side, Kevin carrying his roll of maps, they crossed the tracks and tramped the winding road between the mining buildings until they came to the big frame office building. As usual, because he held the authority between them, Kevin went in first. The door faced a counter, behind which were half a dozen desks and a huge wall safe, its doors open. To their right were two open doors, one on either side of the counter.

A young man wearing sleeve garters and an eye-shade came out of his chair behind the nearest desk, walked up to them and said pleasantly, "Who are you looking for?"

"Your super, Mr. Magruder," Kevin said.

The clerk pointed with his pencil to the door farthest from him and said, "He's in there. Go on in."

Kevin, with Will trailing, went to the doorway and knocked on the wood of the doorframe to announce his presence. They walked into a big, well-lit office containing two roll-top desks. The room was carpeted and held two leather-covered easy chairs facing the desk, at which a burly man in shirt sleeves was sitting. At their entrance he turned his head to look over his shoulder. His was a broad face, surly with authority, and his black eyebrows, under closely cropped grey hair, were the size of ordinary mustaches.

Kevin moved toward the desk and halted, saying, "You're Mr. Magruder?"

Magruder had swiveled his chair to face them. Now Will could see his heavy body, thick legs, and broad hands that had been formed by shovel handles and single-jacks a long time ago.

Kevin had his mouth open to introduce himself when Magruder said, "Lloyd and Christie. I wondered when you'd be around."

"We telegraphed you we'd be here today," Kevin said equably.

Magruder waved to the chairs. "Sit down, if you like." When both had seated themselves Magruder said, "You've come to inspect us, haven't you?"

"Those are my orders," Kevin said.

Magruder looked at Will. "And you're the deputy marshal that backs him up. Have I got that right?"

Will only nodded, studying this forceful man who was already dominating this exchange.

Magruder asked then, "How long have you fellows been traveling?"

"About two weeks," Will said.

"You've been out of touch with the State House, then?" At Will's nod Magruder swiveled his chair, reached for a sheaf of papers, leafed over a couple of them and cleared his throat. "This is from our man in Granite Forks. He says last Monday Alex Hanson, minority leader in the House, introduced a new Mine Inspection bill. It calls for a ten-man Mining Commission to be appointed by the Governor, and answerable only to him. It also calls for the hiring of fifteen mine inspectors answerable only to the commission." He looked up at Will and said, as he extended the sheet he'd been summarizing, "Like to read it?"

Will took it and read it. While Magruder's briefing interested him, the written word angered him. The bill would cut Brady out of the picture, which was the sole intent, he guessed. He passed it over to Kevin, then said to Magruder, "They haven't voted on it yet."

"Oh my, no." Magruder consulted the top sheet. "It's been referred to a conference committee of both Houses."

"Then until it's voted on and passed, the old statute is still in effect," Will said.

"In theory yes, in practice no," Magruder said pleasantly.

Will was silent a moment, then asked, "Will you explain that to us?"

"Our lawyer is asking for a restraining order against Cope."

Will looked at Kevin, who was watching him. "On what grounds?" Will asked.

"Unfairness, let's say. At the rate you and Lloyd are moving, it'll take you three years to inspect all mines. If you find anything wrong with us we have four months to repair it. *And* we'll be inspected a second and likely a third time before you've finished inspecting all the other mines. We're out of pocket while other mines aren't." He added simply, "I wouldn't advise inspecting us now."

"We have the right to until Hanson's bill is passed —if it ever is," Kevin said.

"You may have the right to inspect, but you won't." He heaved his bulk out of his chair and moved over to a window. "Come and look."

Will and Kevin rose and came up behind him. Magruder pointed. "See those two men on either side of the door of the hoist shack? See their rifles?" His finger tilted up. "See the mouths of Two and Three? See the men guarding them with rifles?"

They looked, and the men were there. Magruder went back and settled into his chair before saying,

"Nobody gets in the Mary E except the men that work there. If you want to get underground here, ask the Governor to call out the militia."

Will turned away from the window first and halted in front of Magruder. "Your orders?"

Magruder moved his big head from side to side. "Clay Hatcher, chairman of the board. If you get a letter from him passing you into the mine, I'll honor it."

Will felt a quiet fury—and a sense of total helplessness. The arrogance and the supreme confidence of Magruder told him he had been coached by Hatcher himself. The hell with the law if it didn't suit the Mary E. The mine would make its own laws—was making them in the legislature and defying the present law until they got their own.

He tried to control his voice as he asked, "How do I find Hatcher?"

"He's got a ranch up in the San Dimas. The CH connected."

Will gestured to Kevin and they both left the building without saying good-bye to Magruder.

They halted outside the door, looked at the guarded shaft house and tunnels. Will couldn't be sure, but it seemed as if every man and guard in sight knew who they were and was watching them.

"I've got the feeling this one we'll skip," Kevin said.

"Not without an argument," Will said grimly. "Why don't you go over to the Bullseye and get yourself a drink, and I'll join you there?"

Kevin nodded and they parted, Kevin heading for the saloon and Will for the depot and its telegraph. As he tramped toward the depot he tried to frame the wording of the telegram he was about to send Brady. He thought of a couple of ways to disguise the message so that Cope would understand it and the operator would not, and then he reflected that this was absurd. The operator would get a copy of his message to Magruder immediately, and no matter how cleverly he disguised the contents Magruder would know that Will had only one reason for getting in touch with Cope, that reason being the Mary E.

At the counter of the ticket office on the track side of the dirty waiting room Will asked for a blank and sent this message:

ACCESS TO MARY E DENIED BY MAGRUDER AND GUNMEN STOP HATCHER'S PERMISSION TO INSPECT IS REQUIRED STOP WILL SEE HIM IF YOU ORDER ME STOP PLEASE ADVISE IN CARE OF MINERAL CITY HOTEL FULL STOP SIGNED WILL CHRISTIE

The operator read it without expression, counted the words, and told Will the cost. Will paid up and went out, heading for the Bullseye.

The Bullseye was far less crowded than it had been when he had been there previously. The big houseman who had tossed Costigan out into the street recognized him, came over and they shook hands. Will ordered a whiskey and water from a bartender, waited for it, then carried it over to the table where Kevin was seated.

"All right, what's your argument?" Kevin said as if they hadn't even parted.

"A summons for Clay Hatcher," Will said.

Kevin allowed himself one of his rare smiles. "One of the richest men in the state gets a summons from a deputy—if they let us see him."

"Not us, Kevin. Just me."

Kevin looked at him in bewilderment. "Why not me?"

"Well, if there's trouble I don't want you in it," Will said. "That's not what you're paid for. I am."

Kevin swore and shook his head. "Before you came in here I got to thinking. If we ride out there tomorrow and you give Clay Hatcher a summons, it's worth all the money I've made on this trip just to see his face."

Will smiled, took a drink, looked out at the street and thoughtfully rubbed the bridge of his nose. He knew how Kevin felt, for in Kevin's place he would have felt the same way. It was not often a man got to

76

see the mighty tumble, especially the mean mighty such as Clay Hatcher. Not that Will was sure he would or could humble Hatcher, but one thing was certain: he would get no letter from Hatcher for permission to inspect the Mary E. How Hatcher, who was reputed to be a man of violent temper, would react to being issued a summons was anybody's guess.

Will looked at Kevin and relented. "All right. Come along. Only it's my party, my friend. You stay out of it."

It was very late that night and the town was asleep as three riders abreast came down the main street.

They pulled up their tired horses in front of the Mineral City Hotel. A big man on the horse closest to the hotel swung out of the saddle, crossed to the boardwalk, climbed the hotel porch steps and tested the closed door. By custom, the lobby doors were never locked, in order to accommodate late-hour gamblers and drinkers.

The big man walked carefully toward the low-burning lamp at the desk so as not to disturb the sleeping night clerk, who might be anywhere about. The hotel register lay on the desk.

The night visitor leafed through it until he came to the first blank page and then he worked backwards, scanning the last dozen signatures before he found what he wanted. He closed the book and quietly left the lobby. Out in the street once again, he halted by his horse.

"They're here," he said, and mounted.

16

Will and Kevin left Twin Buttes before daylight. They didn't take the pack horse with them since they would have to return to Twin Buttes to receive Brady's instructions. Just before going to bed last night Will had made out a summons for Clay Hatcher. It was now in his hip pocket.

Will knew that if the serving of the summons was to be legal it must be served on Hatcher himself, and this part had him mildly bothered. All Hatcher had to do to avoid accepting the summons was to instruct his men to say he was absent. This, Will knew, would turn into a hide-and-seek game that could last for a year, or as long as Hatcher wanted it to. And Will had no doubt that Magruder had sent a rider out last night to the CH warning Hatcher to expect a visit.

When daylight came, Will saw they were traveling in a different sort of country from that which they had ridden through yesterday. The saguaro was gone and the mesquite was higher and thicker. As the day came on they could make out the distant San Sabras and saw that the land was gaining height the further east they traveled.

When they pulled up their horses to blow them after a climb of interminable switchbacks that eased the grade of the wagon road they were traveling, Will stepped out of the saddle and said to Kevin, "There's shade over there. Let's chew this over."

78

They led their horses to the shade of a towering pepper tree and sat down together.

Will told Kevin what was on his mind. Last night while Kevin had been bringing his notes up to date in his room, Will had gone back to the Bullseye and talked at some length with the houseman. From him, he had gotten a rough idea of the layout of the CH. He passed this on to Kevin and then changed the subject by saying, "I don't think we ought to go in there together, Kevin."

At Kevin's look of surprise, Will went on to put into words his thoughts of this morning. Almost certainly, he went on to say, they would be barred from seeing Clay Hatcher, or lied to regarding his whereabouts.

"If you show up without me I think he might see you," Will said. "Make it plain you have no power to serve papers on anyone. You're simply out to get the chairman's report on the Mary E cave-in."

"He knows I'll know what happened," Kevin objected.

"So tell him Magruder won't let us in the mine to even have a look. You've just come to the horse's mouth to get the facts for your official report."

Kevin thought about this for several moments, then he looked at Will and asked, "While you do what?"

"Come in the back way," Will answered. "I'll watch to see if you're let in. If you are, that means Hatcher's there. I got a rough idea of the layout of the house last night."

"Sure you don't want to wait until dark? It's risky, Will. Anybody sees you, they'll shoot. Even if they don't shoot at you, the noise will warn the house."

"It's a chance," Will conceded.

Kevin pondered all this, then said, "He'll ask why I ain't with you."

"I'm hanging around town waiting for word from Cope. He'll already know what my telegram said."

"Well, what the hell will I talk to him about?" Kevin asked.

"I don't think you'll do much of the talking, Kevin.

He'll want to know every mine we've been through, and what their reaction was. If he clams up, keep yarning about that."

Kevin shook his head. "Why did I ever think I'd like this?"

"You'll see what you came to see," Will said. "That's enough."

They mounted again, and in another hour they had climbed the foothills of the San Dimas. Here they passed an occasional feeder road coming in from the south, and Will figured these roads led to other ranches. This was borne out presently when they saw a wooden sign on the feeder road bearing the name Moffitt, and under it Box M burned into it with a branding iron. There were no roads coming in from the north, and Will guessed the vast stretch of piñon and grama-grass country in that direction must be CH range. They confirmed this a half-hour later when, coming over a rise, they spooked half a dozen cows bearing the CH brand on their left hip.

Will reined in, and Kevin did too.

"Here's where we split up, Kevin," Will said. "Take your time. I've got two sides of a triangle to travel while you've only got one. The houseman said you could see Hatcher's spread to your left from this road."

Kevin muttered, "Like they say, *Vaya con Dios.*"

Kevin put his horse in motion, while Will pulled off the road and angled north. Kevin rode on slowly for another couple of miles and then over a rise he caught sight of the CH, ahead of and below him. It had to be Hatcher's spread because of the size of the big adobe main house, putting him in mind of an army fort. Huge cottonwoods in the patio almost, but not quite, obscured his view of the north side of the building. The long bunkhouse to the east was of adobe too, while the barns and wagon sheds to the north of the bunkhouse were of timber. A series of corrals that flanked the barns looked out on a vast fenced pasture where horses were grazing.

Awed and a little fearful at what he was walking

into, Kevin went on down the road until he came to the CH turnoff. On either side were huge cedar and piñon trees which, as he came nearer the house, ended abruptly to make room for a big blacksmith shop whose double doors were propped open. As he approached he could hear men talking. When he came abreast of the doors, a man came off the stump stool he was sitting on and, rifle hanging from his right hand, stepped outside the building. He was a tall, gangling, weather-brown man wearing the sun-faded Levi's and denim shirt of a working puncher.

Kevin reined in and the tall man came up to him, halted and said, "You lost, mister?" in a pleasant enough tone of voice.

"I don't think I am if this is the CH."

The puncher regarded him closely, noting his beard, the ancient black hat and worn boots.

"It is. Just who're you looking for?"

"Mr. Clay Hatcher."

"What's your business with him?" the puncher asked.

"I'll tell *him*," Kevin answered.

"No, you'll tell me, I reckon," the puncher said flatly.

They eyed each other with sudden and mutual dislike.

Kevin sighed, indicating he was tolerating a fool. "Mining business," he said.

"Mr. Hatcher's got a mine. I don't reckon he needs another one," he said.

"I'm not selling anything. I just need to talk to him," Kevin said.

"What about?"

Kevin took a deep breath. "Look, I'm a mine inspector by trade. I want to have a look at the Mary E."

"See Magruder."

"I've seen him," Kevin said shortly. "Now, I want to see Mr. Hatcher."

"I don't reckon you do."

Slowly, Kevin reached in his shirt pocket for his

notebook and the stub of a pencil. He wrote on the sheet, tore it out of the notebook and extended it to the puncher. "That's my name. Now, what's yours?"

The puncher took the paper, read Kevin's name and said, "What do you want with my name?"

"For my report to my boss, the Attorney General."

"What'll it get you?"

"It won't get me anything. It might get you something, though."

"Like what?"

"A court summons, say," Kevin said quietly. "I can't issue you one; I can't issue anybody one. All I can say is that you wouldn't let me talk to Mr. Hatcher."

The puncher thought long moments, watching him, then he stuffed the paper Kevin had given him into his shirt pocket. He said, "Stay," and turned and walked toward the big house in the near distance.

Kevin dismounted and looked inside the blacksmith shop. Only then did he see the man the puncher had seen talking to. Here was another puncher, and he, too, held a rifle.

Kevin saw the first puncher step through a double door in the house-high wall of adobe. He was gone a good ten minutes, during which Kevin speculated on how Will could get past the guards he was sure to meet. There were men down at the corrals and a couple of men talking outside the bunkhouse. Hell, there were men everywhere.

He heard a shrill whistle, looked over the wall gate and saw the puncher waving him over.

Kevin got on his horse, rode over to him and dismounted. There were rings in the adobe wall and Kevin tied his horse to one of them.

"Come along," the puncher said.

Kevin stepped through the double-doored gateway and was immediately in the flower-filled patio garden beneath the big cottonwoods. There were several doors on all three sides of the big patio. The guard turned left, walked up to a blue-painted carved door that stood ajar and knocked on it; when he was answered he pushed the door open. He stood aside, shifted his rifle from his right hand to his left and motioned Kevin to precede him.

Kevin entered a big corner room that seemed at first glance to be both library and office. Three walls were lined ceiling-high with books. There was a big desk by a west window. Kevin looked around him. In the corner on his left was a huge sofa covered in red velvet; a round table separated the sofa from two easy chairs facing it.

A grey-haired man wearing casual range clothes tossed some papers he had been reading on the table and rose as the puncher said from behind Kevin, "This is Mr. Lloyd, Mr. Hatcher."

Hatcher was a tall man, thin to gauntness. There was a chill in his grey eyes as he moved over to Kevin and extended his hand. He had a blade of a high-bridged nose that, considered with his lean, deeply tanned face, made Kevin wonder if he wasn't looking at an Indian.

They shook hands and Hatcher said to the puncher, "That's all, Charlie. Thank you." Then he gestured to one of the easy chairs.

Battered hat now in hand, Kevin took the nearest chair and Hatcher seated himself on the red sofa, lifted his legs, crossed them and put his booted feet on the table.

"Been expecting you, Lloyd. Where's your partner?"

The question was so abrupt and to the point that it caught Kevin unprepared, but an evasive answer might suffice. "He's waiting for a telegram," Kevin said. "He'll be along later. Anyway, I don't reckon I'll need him."

Hatcher nodded. "You want into the Mary E to inspect it. Magruder told you to get a letter of permission from me, didn't he? Well, I'm not going to give you one."

In two brief exchanges Kevin's business was done, he realized. He had received curt treatment before and had handed some of it out himself, but he had never heard anything that approached this.

Kevin said quietly, "All right."

"Now tell me what mines you've inspected. How were you received in all of them?"

So Kevin began to talk.

On his roundabout way to the CH, Will rounded up half a dozen CH steers and drove them ahead of him. When he came to a rise and could see the house he saw he had come up the north side of the horse pasture. A couple of hands were rounding up some horses and driving them into the corral. It didn't take long for them to spot him and the cattle he was driving.

When he was sure he'd been seen, he abandoned the cattle and rode the fenceline toward the corrals. A puncher who had been observing the horses being driven into the corral now shifted his attention to Will, who pesently reined up beside him.

The puncher was a middle-aged man gone to belly. His broad unshaven face held an expression of puzzlement.

"Morning," Will said pleasantly.

The puncher nodded, then gestured loosely toward the end of the horse pasture. "Why you driving our stock?" he asked Will, more curious than hostile.

Will lazily thumbed his Stetson back off his forehead and said, "Well, Moffitt over at Box M shipped some stuff day before yesterday. I'm the new brand inspector and we found five head of yours mixed up with his. I rode over with the Box M crew as far as the turnoff. I was coming this way so I offered to deliver them here."

"Funny how those damned critters will leave good grass for no grass at all, but sometimes they do," the puncher said. "We're obliged to you."

"Mr. Hatcher here?" Will asked idly.

"Reckon he is. Why?"

There was no suspicion in the man's expression, and Will said, "In a thing like this I always like an owner's receipt. That's to show that I didn't drive them over into the next county and sell them."

"Makes sense," the puncher said. He turned and

84

started walking past the barns and bunkhouse while Will walked his horse beside him.

They passed the bunkhouse and turned right along the wall and Will saw Kevin's horse standing hip-shot in the shade.

He dismounted and followed the puncher through the gate and watched him turn left, heading for the blue-painted door in the corner, where he knocked.

The puncher was told to enter, and as he moved into the room, Will behind him, he saw Hatcher in the corner seated on the red sofa.

After giving them a glance of both puzzlement and irritation, Hatcher asked, "What is it, Pete?"

"Brand inspector, Mr. Hatcher."

Will was observing this pleasant room as Hatcher said with quiet ferocity, "I do one thing at a time, Pete, and I'm not finished. Wait outside."

Pete turned so abruptly he bumped into Will, who backed away and followed the big-bellied puncher out into the patio, closing the door behind him. Pete looked at Will, shrugged, smiling faintly, and put his heavy back against the wall.

Will's glance roved the patio. There were *portales* on all three sides of the big building, with flagstone walkways. Idly, Will started a slow stroll along the *portal*, hands in hip pockets. Approaching an open window on his left, he assumed this would look on Hatcher's bedroom. Was he married, Will wondered. Then he remembered Brady's remark about the Mary E. He looked in the window and saw a spacious bedroom. There was a big bed against the far wall; some ten feet inside the window was a tall carved wardrobe. Between it and the window was a wooden filing cabinet, and as he passed Will could see a metal bar which ran down the drawer pulls and was attached atop the cabinet with two padlocks.

Because he had seen only one file cabinet that was locked in this manner he remembered where he had seen it. It was in the office of Hugh Evans.

Will did not even pause in his slow stride, but his

mind was in a turmoil. What was Hatcher doing with Evans' missing private files? Then he made the connection. Evans was party chairman and Hatcher was a heavy contributor.

Will sauntered on, looking across the patio to the opposite wing, and realized it was probably the dining and kitchen area. He halted briefly, then turned and slowly began to retrace his steps, as if killing time. As he approached the bedroom window again he did not even turn his head to look at the file cabinet, but he saw it plainly. There was no doubt in his mind now. It was there, unchanged, defying tampering, just as it has been in Hugh Evans' office. He continued his pacing, looked at Pete, who was rolling a smoke, and then turned back again toward Pete, the picture, he hoped, of a man aimlessly walking about with time on his hands.

He had almost reached Pete when the door opened and Kevin stepped out. He shook hands with Hatcher standing in the doorway and said, "You won't change your mind, Mr. Hatcher?"

"No. No letter, Mr. Lloyd."

"Then, good day to you, sir," Kevin said.

He did not even look at Will as he passed.

"Come in, Pete," Hatcher said.

Again Pete led the way and Will pulled his hands from his pockets, took off his hat and followed Pete into the room. Hatcher was moving across to the red sofa, Pete and Will after him. Hatcher sat down, leaned back and said, "Now, what is it, Pete?" in a tone of meager patience.

"Excuse me, Mr. Hatcher, but this fellow's the new brand inspector. Box M shipped day before yesterday. Him and the crew found five head of our stuff mixed in with theirs. He brought 'em back. He wants your signed receipt that he delivered 'em."

Hatcher looked closely at Will and said, "I know you, don't I?"

"I doubt it, Mr. Hatcher. I just got shifted from down south."

Noting the pencil on the table, Will reached in his back pocket, brought out a folded piece of paper, moved to the table and said, "Just scribble it on here, Mr. Hatcher. It's just protection for me."

Hatcher swung his feet down and slowly leaned over the table to pick up the pencil.

"Your name?" he asked.

"Unfold the paper. It's in there," Will said.

Hatcher did. It was the court summons Will had filled out and signed last night. Pete, who had shown Will in twice, silently left the room.

As soon as Hatcher read the summons his face flushed with anger. "I remember that name. You're Joe Isom's boy."

"Isom's friend," Will corrected.

Will watched Hatcher carefully as he said, "That means what is says, Mr. Hatcher. If you don't show up, we'll come and get you. That is, unless you've changed your mind and want to give Kevin what he needs."

Hatcher came to his feet and crushed the summons in his hand. He said flatly, "Damned if I will! You and Lloyd are a couple of ringers paid by Cope."

Then he straightened out the summons and read, " 'You will appear on November 1st,' this says." He tossed the summons back on the table. "By that date Cope won't have a mine inspector. And I'll give you ten-to-one odds that the court voids all the actions you've taken against the mines you've already inspected. Now, get out!"

Kevin was waiting beside his horse when Will approached. He halted and Kevin asked, "You give him the summons?"

Will nodded. "He didn't like it much."

"Damn, and I missed it."

Will went on to explain what had happened after Kevin had left. Then Kevin asked, "You figure he's right, Will?"

"I think he's got money enough to buy anything he wants," Will answered glumly.

They watered their horses at the corral tank and

aftewards headed south past the outbuildings to pick up the Twin Buttes road. Both men were depressed, but Will still felt the residue of excitement—his discovery of the Evans files.

He had already decided not to tell Kevin of the discovery of the missing files, much as he was tempted to. Kevin was wholly unconnected with the theft of the files, so why burden him with unneeded knowledge that might be dangerous?

Now Will wondered how the files could be retrieved. A safer place to hide them than this remote, heavily guarded ranch house couldn't be found. It was foolish to think they could be taken by force unless it was legal force, and only Brady could provide that.

He reflected that even though his ruse to get to Hatcher had worked without a hitch, it seemed that it now counted for nothing. The correspondence he had read in Magruder's office yesterday, together with what Hatcher had told him back at the CH, combined to insure an ominous future for Brady's and Joe's plans. Even if the issue of a new Mining Commission was not yet settled when Hatcher appeared in court, he would pay a fine and appeal it. It could take months while the legislature carpentered and passed a Mining Commission bill that would be mired in politics forever.

They reached Twin Buttes around dusk and went directly to the feed stable. They rode under the archway, and the hostler left half a dozen men in the office to come and take their horses. Will asked that they be grained and stabled tonight, along with the pack horse out in the corral, since they would be leaving before daylight. He paid the hostler the feed bill for the horses.

As they passed the stable office they saw a big, rough-looking man with a match in his mouth leaning his heavy shoulder against the doorframe. He seemed to be looking at something in the street and as they passed him he looked at them without interest in his mud-colored eyes.

On the street Will told Kevin to go on to the Bulls-eye while he checked at the depot for an answer to his telegram. The big man in the stable office watched them separate, then strolled back down the runway and halted at the far door. He watched the hostler tie the two thirsty horses to the water trough, then pick up a halter and enter the corral, which held a dozen horses. The hostler isolated a sturdy-looking bay from the others, put a halter on him, led him out of the corral and into the stable, where he stalled him. The big man noted that this horse had the same brand as the horses drinking at the trough.

Presently, the hostler retraced his steps and led the horses back to the stable. There he stalled them too, unsaddled them and fed them. All this the big man noted without really watching. It was a fairly simple deduction that his quarry was planning a before-daylight start in the morning; stabling his horses tonight would save cutting them out from the other horses in the corral by lantern light in the morning. Since he had seen Christie give the hostler money for the feed bill he didn't even need to talk to the hostler to confirm his own judgment. Walking through the stable, he hit the street and, turning right, walked down to one of the sleazy saloons fronting the railroad tracks.

At the depot Will waited at the wicket until the agent finished a message on the key and came to the counter.

"Anything today for Will Christie?"

"I sent it with the boy to the hotel. I can tell you what it said, though. It read, 'Forget Hatcher. Come home,' and it was signed, 'Brady Cope.' "

Will thanked him, put a quarter on the counter, saying, "That's for the boy."

On the way to the Bullseye he thought about Brady's message. According to their planned itinerary, the Mary E was the last mine to be inspected. What puzzled Will was Brady's reason for telling him to forget Hatcher. It was too late to forget him and he'd been served a summons, but still it didn't satisfy Will's curiosity. Was there trouble shaping up at Granite Forks so that Brady wanted him there? He couldn't know.

He found Kevin at a table in the Bullseye, which was crowded with miners off the dayshift. Kevin had already ordered both drinks and Will sat down behind his.

"Well, Brady's called us home, Kevin. His telegram said to forget Hatcher." He took a deep drink of his whiskey.

"But he's got him where he wants him," Kevin protested. Then he said, "Of course, he don't know that yet."

They finished their drinks and Will rose. It was almost dark on the street, and he said, "I'll go pick up some grub before the store closes. Go get your supper and I'll be along later."

17

In the chill of the dark early morning the man who had been leaning against the doorframe of the deserted dark Bullseye saloon came erect. He crossed the boardwalk, ducked under the tie rail where three horses were tethered and crossed the empty street. He mounted the steps, and by the dim light from the lobby lamp made out the two figures seated side by side on the porch chairs.

"Right-hand corner room you told me," he said.

"Yeah,"

"They just lit the lamp," the watcher said.

"All right, get on the other side of the door. Remember, it's the tall one we want. You keep your gun on the other man."

For ten minutes the three men on the porch sat in silence, listening. Presently, when they heard the sound of bootheels making a subdued racket on the stairs, the big man rose. He lifted his chair by the back, turned it upside down and raised it so an arm of the chair rested on his shoulders. Then he moved as close to the wall as he could get.

The sound of footsteps became louder, then halted, and the far section of the half-glassed doors swung inward. Kevin, carrying a half-filled burlap sack of grub, stepped onto the porch, heading for the steps.

Will, a pace behind him, also stepped out, closing the door behind him. He heard a faint, whistling sound to his left that he couldn't even try to identify before something crashed down on his head and shoulders with a violence that drove him to his knees. Off balance, blinded by the pinwheels of pain, he fell forward on his face.

Kevin, hearing the sound of the blow and shattering of the chair, wheeled to look behind him and saw Will fall. Before Kevin could move, a man with a drawn gun came out of the darkness to his left and was silhouetted against the lobby lamplight. A huge man stepped out of the darkness to the right and gave Will a savage kick in the side. Even as he watched him, Kevin felt the gun barrel in his own belly.

The big man leaned over Will and was lifting him to his feet when a third man moved out of the darkness to the right and into the faint lamplight. He faced Will, and Kevin saw that he had a wide leather belt wrapped around his fist. He drove that belted hand at Will's hanging head and it made a sound that almost sickened Kevin.

Wild with anger now, Kevin swung the sack of grub at the head of the man with the gun. He felt and heard it hit, and then the gun went off.

Kevin felt a tearing blow in his leg that drove him

backwards with numbing force until he missed his footing and fell on his back down the steps.

He lay there for dazed moments, silently cursing the fact that both his leg and his head hurt and that Will needed him. He could hear all right, but could only move slowly, and could see nothing, because he was head down on the steps. What he heard was the sound of bone meeting flesh, and then a different sound; something heavy enough to make a small and different racket came tumbling down the steps and stopped beside his shoulder.

Painfully he rolled over on his side, slid his body down the two remaining steps and looked at what had touched his shoulder. Reaching for it, he found it was a six-gun. He hefted it with no comprehension why it was there. It took him only seconds to understand that it was very likely Will's gun, which had been taken from his holster and tossed aside out of Will's possible reach.

The beating ended with the sound of Will's body falling on the porch. Above the deep breathing of the men who had beset them came the sound of someone running across the lobby toward the door.

One of the men on the porch above said brusquely, "Let's get out of here," in a commanding tone of voice.

Kevin cocked the gun in his hand and lay still. Two men hurtled down the steps and passed him. Then the big man appeared in silhouette, heading after them in a hurry too.

Kevin raised his gun, saw the big man would trample him, and pulled the trigger.

On the very heels of the shot he heard the wind driven from the man's lungs in a strangled bellow, and then the big man fell on him in a tumbling crash that knocked Kevin onto the sidewalk before the big body rolled over him, came to a halt, giving a wet bubbling sigh, and was still.

Kevin heard the sound of a pair of horses at a dead gallop down the dark street. He waited, fully conscious but too tired to move. His left leg and his belly were wet with his blood.

Presently a light appeared above him on the porch and when Kevin turned to look he saw the night clerk in a long nightshirt appear at the edge of the porch, lamp in hand, looking down at him.

"Help me up," Kevin said. No sound came, he realized, and then he shouted, "Help me up." The shout turned out to be only a mutter, but the night clerk heard. He set the lamp on the edge of the porch, came down and, frail old man that he was, managed to get Kevin on his feet and put his arm around his own neck. Together they lurched up the steps and when they were on the porch Kevin saw Will sprawled face down, arms spread, blood pooling around him in the kindling of the smashed chair.

Kevin staggered toward the nearest chair, slacked into it and said, "Go knock on rooms. Get some help."

The clerk picked up the lamp and hurried back into the lobby, while Kevin pulled off his belt, maneuvered it around his leg above where it hurt and drew it as tight as he could. Will lay ten feet from him and was still. Kevin tried to hoist himself to his feet but could not because his arms, no matter how hard he struggled, would not move his weight off the seat of the chair. The bitter thought came to him that while he watched, helpless as a baby, Will might be dying.

He did not know whether it was a minute or ten when his hands, too weak to hold the tourniquet, gave up on him and he fainted.

When he came to, it was from the shock of cold water thrown in his face. The first thing he saw was a swarm of men on the porch attending Will, and more down on the sidewalk. All the men he could see were barefoot, with pants pulled up over their underwear. Others hadn't bothered to put on pants.

Now four men lifted Will off the floor and carried him inside. Kevin could hear the men saying, "Easy does it," "Now take it easy," "Whoa," "Watch that arm," "Keep his head up," and such talk. Now two other men seized the legs of the chair Kevin was sitting on and carried him in the chair into the lobby. Someone had found a piece of the splintered chair out on the porch and with it had tightened his tourniquet.

Will, preceding him, was carried into a gound-floor room that held two beds. When Kevin was carried into the room Will was already on one of them and Kevin got a glimpse of his bloody, battered face.

He himself was lifted out of the chair and stretched out on the other bed. Someone he had never seen before leaned over the bed and said, "They've gone after the doc."

18

Deputy Sheriff John Thompson's office was around the corner from the Bullseye saloon and two doors south. It was a paint-peeled frame building that had once housed a business long since failed. The room opening off the street was the office, which held a rolltop desk with swivel chair against the south wall, a straight-backed chair next to the desk and facing the room, and an easy chair leaking stuffing against the opposite wall. Farther back in the building was a two-celled jail and the deputy's living quarters.

This mid-morning, Deputy Sheriff Thompson, his coat and hat thrown on the easy chair, was slacked wearily into the swivel chair facing the desk. His white hair was mussed up, and he was still wearing his nightshirt of red cotton flannel tucked into his pants.

He was contemplating the notes he had made earlier with something like loathing on his handsome face. He was about to take on the chore he hated most—writing the report of last night's beatings and killing. He might as well get at it while it was still fresh in his mind, he thought. He pulled open the left-hand drawer of his desk, took out a fresh piece of paper, and was fumbling around in the drawer for a pencil when he heard the front door open.

Glancing up, he identified his caller and groaned softly.

A young man in shirt sleeves entered, carrying a tablet in his left hand. He closed the door with his right, and then plucked a pencil from his shirt pocket as he came over to the desk and without an invitation sat down in the straight-backed chair. He had, the sheriff thought sourly, the face of an intelligent pig; his nostrils were wide and uptilted, his jaw a little undershot, and when he spoke it was in a high, squeaky voice.

"It's about time I got around to you, Sheriff." Lennie Piersall was a clerk at the Emporium General Store, but he was also a stringer for Phil Costigan's *Granite Forks Herald*.

"Who else is there to get around to but me?" the sheriff asked.

Piersall opened his tablet, found his last notes and then said, "Why, Doc Kelly, and the night man Bogardus and the hotel guests that helped, and then I had to look at the corpse." He looked up. "Whose is it?"

With an effort Thompson leaned forward and with a finger stirred a pile of coins, a knife, a dozen horseshoe nails, a half-plug of lint-covered tobacco, a worn and greasy snap purse and a wrinkled and dirty piece of paper.

He lifted the paper and was unfolding it when Piersall asked, "That his stuff?"

Thompson only nodded.

"Aren't those double eagles?"

"Seem to be," Thompson said calmly.

"What's a saddle tramp like him doing with that kind of money?"

"I couldn't ask him," Thompson said.

"How much is there?"

"Over a hundred fifty dollars," Thompson said.

Now he smoothed out the paper he held in his hands and said, "This here's a bill of sale for a horse. It's made out to Tom Riordan." He looked at Piersall. "It lists a three-year-old bay gelding branded WW. The horse was tied in front of the Bullseye saloon when I got there." Piersall wrote all this down, then asked, "Who signed the bill of sale?"

Thompson extended the paper. "You figure it out."

Piersall looked at the bill of sale, saw that the signature was unreadable and tossed it back on the desk.

"Why'd he beat up Christie?"

"He didn't say," Thompson answered drily.

Piersall cheerfully overlooked the sarcasm and observed, "When Christie comes to, maybe he'll know."

"Maybe. Lloyd don't, though."

"The other two men—you know anything about them?"

"Nope."

"You try and track their horses?"

"Uh huh. They took the road south toward Loma. By the time we got around to track 'em we run into three ore wagons. They camped last night just short of town. We met 'em on the road. Their teams had taken care of any tracks."

"Did you look on the road past their camp?"

"We did. No sign."

"You got any statement to make for the *Herald*?"

"What statement did I make the last time something like this happened?"

Piersall looked at the ceiling. "You said, 'Investigation under way.' "

"Then say it again," Thompson said.

"Yoy knew Lloyd was a mine inspector and Christie a deputy state marshal, didn't you?"

Thompson nodded. "I found papers in both of their clothes saying so."

"You don't tie this in with some sorehead mine operator that got inspected?"

"That would be all of them, wouldn't it?" Thompson said wearily. "A lawman gets shot in the night. Everybody he ever arrested is a suspect. Same way now."

Piersall frowned, rummaging in his mind for further questions. Finally he said, "Can I use your back room to write up my story?"

"What's the matter with your own?" Thompson asked.

"I live out on the edge of town, a fifteen-minute walk. Here I'm close to the telegraph."

Sheriff Thompson came slowly to his feet. "Write it here. I'm going to catch some sleep."

When the boy who delivered telegrams for Jess Dunn, the Granite Forks station agent, arrived at Phil Costigan's office, the *Herald*'s editor was seated at his big square desk. He glanced at the three pages of the collect story that Lennie Piersall had sent and was tempted to refuse the charges, since in mid-morning this same lad had summoned Phil to the depot where Jess had told him the telegrapher's gossip of the shoot-out at Twin Buttes. Still, if he wanted to keep Jess friendly he couldn't refuse to pay. He rose, circled the desk, took enough out of the cash drawer to pay for the telegram and then went back to his desk and began to read Piersall's story.

It was a good one. When he came to the name of the man who had been shot dead by Kelvin Lloyd he stopped reading and put down the telegram. Reaching into his top right-hand drawer, he pulled out a list of names, copied from the *Herald* files. These were the names of the men involved in the rustling ring that Joe Isom and Will Christie had helped round up and capture.

In copying the names he had been too lazy to list them alphabetically and now he cursed softly. It was a long list, but he went through it doggedly. There was no Riordan on the list. Maybe, just maybe, the dead man wasn't a blood relative of one of the convicted rustlers; he could have been married to one though, or maybe one or both of the two men who had escaped were blood relatives of one of the rustlers. *A helluva lot of good that does me,* Costigan thought. There was no motive to hang the story on. It wasn't like Frank Jackson or the men who worked for him to foul up like this.

Something occurred to him then and he rose and went over to the counter. Below the countertop were the files of the *Herald.* They were big volumes bound in leather and cardboard covers. On the back of each volume that held all the copies of the *Herald* printed in a year was a pasted card indicating the year.

Costigan well remembered the date of the famous battle of Tres Piedras. He pulled out the volume, set it on the counter and leafed through the yellowing sheets until he came to the mid-October issue. In the biggest block type the *Herald* had the headline proclaimed, "Big Rustling Ring Broken." What he was looking for would be at the end of the story. He turned to the back page carry-over. In a black-bordered box headed, "List of the Identified Dead," the third name was that of Hugh Riordan, age approximately 48. Smiling, he closed the volume and put it back in its place. Silently apologizing to Frank Jackson, he returned to his desk and finished reading the telegram. All in all it was a good story, he thought.

He leaned back in his chair with a feeling of both excitement and pleasure. In his story Lennie Piersall had listed the probable age of the dead Tom Riordan as 42. *Younger brother of Hugh,* Costigan decided. If he was any relative of Hugh Riordan's there was the motive for the beating of Will Christie, and it was a beauty.

He rose, went back in the shop and handed the telegram to his printer. "Set this up and hold it for another take. I'll be back."

He put on his hat and headed downstreet for Frank Jackson's office. If Frank could get hold of his man who had hired Riordan and confirm that Hugh and Tom Riordan were related, then he would be even with Will Christie. No guilt would point to Phil Costigan.

19

It was shortly after eleven when Jim Cousins, Brady's not-so-new secretary by now, went into Brady's office after announcing himself with a knock on the door. Jim was followed by a boy of twelve who held his hat in his hand.

"A gentleman to see you, sir," Jim said to Brady. Cope looked at the boy and smiled.

"How are you this morning, Roy?"

The boy was a familiar figure in the State House; he had even delivered Will's telegram from Twin Buttes.

Now he said, "Mr. Dunn said to ask you if you and Mr. Isom could stop by the depot before dinner."

Brady frowned, and thought immediately that Dunn, by asking for him and Joe, must have news of Will and Kevin. "Go ask Joe, will you, Jim? I'll be out at the hack stand."

Jim left the room and headed for Isom's office. Brady rose and skirted the desk, reached in his pocket, pulled out a coin and gave it to the boy, saying, "Thanks, Roy. We're almost on our way."

As the boy left the room Brady went into the ante-room, took his coat and hat from the hatrack and went out. He was thinking what a benign tyrant Jess Dunn had been over the years. Because he could not leave his telegraph key he could summon anyone in town to the depot when news came over the wire that concerned them in any way. Frank Jackson, Dunn's boss, knew this and encouraged it, although it was strictly against the law.

Outside, Brady waved a hack over to the steps and heard Joe coming down them behind him. They exchanged good mornings and climbed into the hack, and when they were seated Joe observed, "A little bit of fall in the air this morning, Brady."

Brady acknowledged there was, and that ended the conversation. Brady knew that Joe's first reaction to the summons had been like his own, but it seemed useless to speculate at this stage about the meaning of the summons.

Jess Dunn glanced up at their entrance, picked up a sheaf of papers from his desk, opened the door, came out to the waiting room, gave them good morning and gestured toward the hard wooden benches, saying, "Take one of my easy chairs, gentlemen."

All three men sat down and Jess consulted his notes. "This came in a while ago for Costigan," he said. "Thought you might like to know about it. It's from Twin Buttes. Early this morning, way before daylight, your men walked out of the hotel and were jumped on the hotel porch by three men. One, the biggest, crashed a porch chair over Christie's head, knocking him cold. Then he picked Christie up and held him while the second man, his right fist wrapped with a leather belt, proceeded to beat the livin' be-Jesus out of Christie."

He looked up to see if his audience was attentive; they were, and he proceeded.

"A third man put a gun on Lloyd. Lloyd was carrying a sack of grub and he swung it and hit the third man. The gun went off and the bullet hit Lloyd in the leg, knocking him down the steps. One of the men beating Christie took Christie's gun and threw it toward the street. It landed by Lloyd and he picked it up. The gunshot and racket on the porch brought the night man running to the porch. Two of the men ran past Lloyd heading for their horses tied across the street. The last man, the big one, came down the steps and Lloyd shot and killed him. Christie was beat up badly and was still unconscious at the time this telegram was filed. Lloyd lost a lot of blood and they don't know if his thigh bone is shattered. Both your men were carried into a first-floor room of the hotel. They are there now, under the care of Doc Kelly."

He looked up. "That's about it."

Brady looked at Joe. "Why?" he asked.

Joe shook his head, signifying that he didn't know. Then he asked. "Did they identify the dead man?"

Jess consulted his notes again. "Yes. Tom Riordan, address unknown. The sheriff found his name on a horse bill of sale he had in his pocket. The other two men escaped."

"Any mention of them inspecting mines?" Joe asked.

"That's the way the story starts off," Jess said as he looked at his notes. " 'State Mine Inspector Kevin Lloyd and Deputy Marshal Will Christic wcrc attacked by three men before daylight this morning . . .' "

Brady and Joe exchanged glances, and Brady asked, "Any mention of the number of court summonses in Will's possession?"

"No mention," the agent said. Dunn held up the sheaf of papers. "I'd give you these, except they're in my own kind of shorthand. You couldn't read 'em."

Brady looked at Joe. "Anything else you can think of?" he asked. Joe shook his head, and Brady rose.

He extended his hand to the agent, and said. "Thank you for the favor, Jess."

They shook hands and Dunn said, "That kind of news ain't much of a favor. But thought you'd want to know."

Outside the depot Brady halted and drew his watch

from his pocket. "It's close to dinnertime, Joe. Come eat with us at the house."

Joe started to protest about being an unexpected guest, but Brady cut him off with one word. "Nonsense."

The hack dropped them off in front of the Evans house and Brady asked the driver to pick them up in an hour and a half.

As they were going up the walk Joe said, "No use telling Belle about this until we're finished dinner, is there?"

"I think that's best," Brady agreed.

When they went in Belle was in the kitchen, but she heard the front door shut. She came into the living room, saw Joe and said, "So Pa roped you in for dinner, Joe. I keep telling him to bring you, but he says that with Will gone you want to stay close to the office."

Joe nodded. "He talked me out of it today, Belle." He surveyed her with open appreciation and said, "For an overworked housekeeper you look mighty pretty."

"I call that singing for your dinner, Joe, but thank you."

Brady took Joe's hat, and on his way to the hatrack he said, "I think this calls for a noonday drink. I'll make 'em."

He hung up their hats and said, "Sit down, Joe."

Belle went out to set the table and Brady followed her and went out onto the back porch. There he lifted the lid of the icebox, found the icepick, chipped a double handful of ice from the cake there and brought it back to the sink, where he washed it and then made the drinks. All the while he was thinking of what Jess Dunn had read from his notes. Somewhere, somehow, there had to be an explanation for this otherwise senseless attack on his men.

Belle came in and busied herself with what was cooking on the stove. Brady set her weakened drink on the counter and then moved into the living room with the other two drinks.

102

Joe took his drink and went over to the easy chair, while Brady seated himself on the sofa. Joe lifted his glass and said, "To a change of luck for Will and Kevin."

They both drank, and then Joe asked, "Do you think we could pry Doc Price away to go down and have a look at them?"

Brady was about to answer, but then made a covert sign with his hands that silently said, "Turn it off."

Belle, minus her apron, came in carrying her drink and sat down beside Brady. She was wearing a maroon shirtwaist with jet buttons, which contrasted nicely with her chestnut hair.

She sipped on her drink and asked, "How are the hearings going, Pa?"

"I'm scheduled to testify again this afternoon," Brady said. He held up his glass and said, "Maybe that explains this."

They discussed the progress of the committee hearings on the new Mine Inspection bill. Their drinks finished, Belle called them to the table, and went on to serve them dinner. They continued to discuss the hearings during the meal, and afterwards when both men had lit cigars Belle pushed her chair back as if to rise.

"Hold on, Belle. Sit down with us a while," Brady said.

Belle looked from her father to Joe in puzzlement. "You both look pretty damned solemn."

"So will you, Belle," Brady answered, and launched into the account of the attack on Will and Kevin. Belle listened with careful attention, her lips parted in disbelief and dismay.

When Brady had finished she said softly, "Dear God, why was it done to them?"

"Nobody knows," Joe said.

Belle sat utterly motionless for seconds, and then said to her father, "Can you get along for a few days without me, Pa?"

At Brady's questioning look Belle went on, "I'm

103

going down there on this afternoon's train. They'll need nursing, and I'll bet they're not getting it."

Brady and Joe looked at each other; they were nodding at each other.

Brady spoke first. "You're absolutely right, Belle. By all means go."

It was dark when the train pulled up to the depot platform in Twin Buttes. Jim Cousins was first off the long passenger car and he handed Belle down to the platform.

On Brady's return to his office after dinner in Granite Forks he told Jim of Will's and Kevin's beating and of Belle's plan to go to Twin Buttes that evening. It was Jim who reminded Brady that both men would probably be unable to ride for some time and that, with Brady's permission, he could go with Belle to Twin Buttes, pick up the horses and bring them back. Brady had agreed.

Now, Jim climbed back up the coach steps, picked up Belle's valise and his own blanketroll, came down to the platform and joined Belle. As the Mineral City Hotel was within easy walking distance, Jim shouldered his blanketroll, picked up the valise, and he and Belle started out to walk the half-block to the hotel.

From the old grey-haired clerk at the desk Belle learned that the room next to Kevin and Will was vacant, and she took it. After signing the register she asked, "Is Mr. Christie still unconscious?"

"No, he came out of it before noon. He even et some soup."

"How are they both?" Belle asked.

The clerk shrugged. "You'll have to ask Doc Kelly, miss. He said he'd come by after supper."

"Can I see them for a minute just to let them know we're here?"

"Don't see why not. The sheriff's been in a couple of times, and so has the doc. It's room number two. First door on your left." He pointed to the lamplit corridor.

104

Belle looked at Jim, who said, "You go on, Miss Belle. Just tell 'em I'm here. I'll carry your valise down the hall." He picked up her bag and headed for the corridor and Belle fell in behind him.

She wished she could steel herself for what was about to happen. She'd seen badly hurt men before, but somehow this was different, and more important.

She halted before the closed door with the numeral two painted on it and knocked softly. A muffled voice said, "Come in." Belle took a deep quavery breath, palmed the door open and stepped inside the big room.

Will's bed was closest to the door. He was sitting up, pillows propped behind his back, and was stripped to the waist. Oddly, the first thing about him Belle noticed were a dozen ugly bruises above and below the wide bandages circling his chest. Her glance lifted then to his face, bruised and swollen out of shape. One eye was shut, but the other blue eye held a look of surprise and incredulity. Above his left eyebrow was a bandage pad that was stained with new blood and was tied in place by a band of cloth circling his head above his ears.

"Belle," Will said through swollen lips, "what are you doing here?" His hands, unmarked because he had never struck a blow, lay on the coverlet, and now he held out his hand.

They shook hands and Belle said, "Pa sent me down here to make sure you were still alive."

Will tried to smile and it didn't come off, but it moved his upper lip enough to show the cotton stuffed in both nostrils.

"Well, I can remember feeling better," he said.

Belle's glance went to the adjoining bed where Kevin lay stretched out, his head turned to them. Seeing her look, Will said, "Belle, this is my partner, Kevin Lloyd, Kevin, this is Brady's girl, Belle."

Belle moved around Will's bed to Kevin's. He, too, was stripped to the waist, baring a wide chest matted with black hair. A smile broke through his beard and showed teeth of startling whiteness.

He held out his hand and Belle took it. "You, Mr. Lloyd, are the other half of a sorry-looking pair. It's good to meet you at last."

"You're prettier than Will said you were, Miss Belle."

Belle smiled with pleasure. "Well, I'm prettier than he is right now, I think."

There was a knock on the door and a man strolled in. He was short, pot-bellied and ruddy-faced, and was carrying a black bag. She didn't need Will's introduction, for she was sure this was Doc Kelly.

Belle came around the bed. The doctor put his bag on the bed and they shook hands.

"You couldn't be a nurse, could you?" Doc Kelly asked.

"Not a trained one, but I think I can help out some."

Doc Kelly surveyed Will. "You're bleeding again," he remarked. "Those scalp wounds go on forever even if they're sewed up."

He looked at Kevin. "You're the man I want to look at first, Mr. Lloyd." He moved past Belle and started around to Kevin's bed. He had his hand on the covers to pull them back when he halted and looked around at Belle. She understood what he was about to say, and said, "I'm leaving, Doctor. Could I wait for you in the lobby?"

At his nod Belle said, "I'm right next door, Will. If you need me have Kevin knock on the wall. See you tomorrow."

Will tried to smile but couldn't, and lifted his hand in a good-bye gesture.

Out in the hall Belle turned toward her room. She unlocked the door, put her valise inside, then relocked the door and headed for the lobby. On her way, she saw the dining room was still open. She was not only tired from the spine-jolting train ride but was hungry too. Still, she did not want to miss Doctor Kelly, so she sat down in the lobby and waited.

It took the doctor some twenty minutes before he

appeared, looked around and spotted her, came over and sat down beside her on the sofa.

"Young Christie told me who you are," Doc Kelly said. "I know your father. Please give him my regards when you see him next."

The smell of whiskey was on his breath and Belle suspected it was seldom absent from it.

She said, "How badly are they hurt. Doctor?"

"I'm not worried about young Christie. A couple of broken ribs, a gash on his head I sewed up, and a busted nose and just what you saw. Lloyd is something else again. I dug bone splinters out of his wound, but I'll have to wait to go into it until he's in better shape. He's lost a lot of blood."

"Could Will travel by train?" Belle asked.

Doctor Kelly grimaced. "He shouldn't, but he will. You're thinking of Granite Forks, of course?"

At Belle's nod, he said, "Any doctor can change his dressings."

"When can he go?"

Doctor Kelly smiled. "He'll let you know."

Belle thanked him and said good night. At the doorway of the dining room she halted and looked over her shoulder. Doctor Kelly was headed for the hotel's saloon. When she looked into the dining room she saw Jim Cousins wave to her and she made straight for his table.

20

The next morning, not very early, Belle went to the hotel desk first and asked of the same clerk she had seen yesterday, "Is it possible to get breakfast brought to one of the rooms?"

"You mean for Christie and Lloyd, don't you?"

At Belle's nod, the old man smiled. "They were served breakfast as soon as the kitchen opened. They've already finished."

Belle felt a little foolish at the news. She had come down to Twin Buttes to look after them, and her first chore had already been looked after. Retracing her steps to room two, she knocked, waited a few seconds and had her hand raised to knock again when the door was opened by Will. He was dressed in clean range clothes, and except for his battered face and the bandages he looked as fit as ever.

When she had recovered her surprise she shook her head. "I knew this was coming, but I didn't think it would be so soon, Will. How are you?"

She glanced across Will's already made bed and waved to Kevin. "Good morning, Mr. Lloyd." Kevin gave a cheerful good morning and then Will gestured toward one of the easy chairs on either side of the window. Belle sat down and watched Will walk very carefully toward the other chair. He sat down gingerly, holding his breath. She noticed now that the swelling had gone down enough in the blackened eye that the lids were partially open.

She asked, "Wouldn't another day in bed have helped?"

"I've got things to do, Belle. Have you had breakfast?" When she said no, Will pulled himself erect. "I might as well test my legs. Let's get you something to eat." He looked at Kevin. "I'm going out into the big world, Kevin. Anything you want from out there?" Kevin grinned and shook his head.

Belle went slowly into the corridor beside Will, headed for the open doors of the dining room. She noticed perspiration trickling from Will's cheek. She said softly, "You're an idiot, Will. You'll never make it. Let's turn around."

"Let's don't," Will said flatly. "I want to talk to you alone."

They made it to the table of Will's choice, which was at the far end of the room. He was, Belle noticed, pushing himself as close to the limit of his present endurance as he dared.

Once they were seated, a waitress came to their table and Belle ordered breakfast. Will ordered only a cup of coffee, and when the waitress had gone he said, "I'm heading for home today, Belle."

"Riding, I suppose," Belle said drily. Only then did she realize that she had not told Will that Jim Cousins was here to bring back the horses.

"No, the train," Will said. "I'll figure something out about the horses later."

Then Belle told him that Jim Cousins was there to take care of that. When Will nodded approval she added, "You're a maniac, Will. What difference does a couple of days make? Besides, what about Kevin? You can't take him along."

"Doc Kelly will have Kevin moved to a room in his house. He already offered to, but Kevin wanted to be near me. Doc didn't have room for us both, so that's why we're here."

109

The waitress came with Belle's breakfast. She poured a cup of coffee for Will and left.

"You still haven't answered my question. What's the tearing rush to get home?"

"You eat your breakfast while I tell you," Will said. Then as Belle ate, watched him and listened, he told her of his and Kevin's visit to Magruder at the Mary E and their visit to Clay Hatcher's CH, either to get permission or to give Hatcher a summons. He described the ruse which allowed him to confront Hatcher only momentarily before he and the puncher were ordered to wait outside until their turn came to talk to him. He told of his stroll in the patio, and what he had glimpsed through Hatcher's bedroom window.

Belle halted her food-laden fork halfway to her mouth. "You mean the very same file that was stolen from Pa's office?"

Will nodded. He couldn't be sure the file was the same, he said, but Evans' file had been locked in a fashion he had never seen before. His coffee untouched, Will said, "I've got to see your father as soon as I can."

"I can tell him," Belle said.

"So can I, and I can hear how he wants it handled. That's what's important."

Belle finished her breakfast, knowing now that nothing could change Will's mind. He was going home on the train today if he had to be carried on, she knew. Before they rose from the table Will said, "Nothing about this file discovery to Kevin, Belle. He doesn't know, and he shouldn't know. I don't want him set up for a Clay Hatcher revenge."

Belle agreed.

Both Doctor Kelly and Jim Cousins were in the room when she and Will returned. Will immediately slacked onto his bed out of sheer weariness. They discussed Kevin's move to Doc Kelly's, which the doctor said he welcomed because Kevin would be under his close surveillance.

Doctor Kelly had accepted the news of Will's departure with a shrug, and Belle knew he'd been expecting it.

Jim Cousins left to bring a flatbed wagon back to the hotel. When he returned he had three men with him, recruited from the feed-stable loafers. Under the watchful eye of Doctor Kelly, Kevin, after saying good-bye to Will, was carried on his mattress out through the lobby and loaded gently onto the wagon.

The doctor rode in the wagonbed beside Kevin, and flanking the wagon were the three recruits from the stable. Seated beside Jim was Belle. This unlikely procession made its way to Doc Kelly's small frame house at the north edge of town. When the wagon stopped in front of the house, the doctor told Belle how to find the ground-floor bedroom where Kevin would be put. She went through the small waiting room into a hall that led to the kitchen. The first door to her left gave onto a small hot room. After raising the shades and opening the windows for ventilation, she stripped off the blankets. Then she went to the tiny kitchen, found a water pitcher and glass, and brought them back and put them on top of the dresser.

The grunting and hard breathing of the four men carrying Kevin was heard before the men were seen. It took some careful maneuvering to get Kevin's mattress through the door, but they managed it, and placed it on top of the mattress already on the bed. Kevin, though not making a sound, was hurting, and Doctor Kelly knew it. He went into his office and returned with a bottle of laudanum, poured out a small amount and fed it to Kevin.

The men left; Belle made Kevin comfortable and then followed Doctor Kelly into his office. In a brief conversation he promised he would keep in daily touch with her by telegraph as to Kevin's progress.

Outside in the sunshine, Belle headed back down the dusty street toward the center of town. A feeling of inadequacy was nagging her. She had come down here to help take care of two hurt men. Her own private assessment of herself was that she had been foolish. But

111

then she told herself that she would always have felt guilty if she had not come down.

Will was asleep when she entered his room, and she didn't wake him. She tiptoed over to one of the easy chairs and sank into it. The only sound in the room was Will's easy breathing.

Watching him, she remembered the last time they had been together on the ride up to the Cousins place. What was most vivid in her memory and what she would never forget was the heart-stopping meeting with the bear and her cubs. Perhaps Will hadn't realized how helpless and terrified she'd been as she saw the charging mother; nor had he realized that in his wildly reckless but sensible way out of the trouble, his strong arm holding her, she had temporarily blacked out. When he had put her down she had feigned a composure she did not feel. Another thing she would never forget was his offhand, self-deprecatory dismissal of the whole incident. He was, she thought, very much of a man. The serving of the summons on Hatcher had again showed his resourcefulness in a tight situation. He was, to put it not so briefly, a brave, kind, strong man, whom she felt she knew better than any other man she had ever known, with the exception of her father. In plain fact, she thought she was more than half in love with him.

Belle and Will waited in the comfortable seat of the hack until the northbound train pulled into the depot. When Belle had bought Will's ticket she had asked the agent to hold the train for them.

Now Will climbed down from the hack, and made the edge of the platform while Belle watched. Together, Will carrying his hat since it would not fit over the bandages, they moved slowly toward the lone passenger car while the other travelers boarded the train. By prearrangement, Belle boarded first and found a pair of double seats facing each other. She placed her valise on the facing seat and then sat down next to the window.

Will made his stiff, slow way down the aisle and

slacked into the seat beside Belle. He was, Belle saw, an object of curiosity to the passengers, who caught an awed glimpse of him.

Once the brakeman saw Will seat himself he stepped down and gave the signal, and the mixed train pulled out into the hot afternoon. Belle looked out the window and wondered how Will would receive the orders he would get from her on the depot platform in Granite Forks.

She became aware of the pressure on her shoulder. She turned her head and saw that Will had fallen asleep and slacked against her. She gently shook him awake, and when his eyes opened he straightened up.

Belle said, "Lie down on the other seat, Will." She rose and put her valise on its side and moved it against the window. Will then moved to the opposite seat and lay down facing her so that the bandage on his cut forehead would be free of the valise. He was asleep in minutes, and stayed that way until two hours later when the train whistled for Granite Forks.

When the train stopped Belle said, "Wait until the others are off, Will. I'll go out now and make sure we have a hack."

Will only nodded and Belle stood up and moved down the aisle ahead of the first passenger. She knew without having to ask that the jolting train ride had both hurt and exhausted Will.

To the driver of the first hack that was empty she said, "Please hold this for me. I've got a hurt man with me." At the driver's nod Belle went back across the platform and saw Will slowly descending the steps.

Once he was in the hack, the driver said, "Where to, ma'am?"

"The Evans house on Grant Street."

Will turned his head to look at her. "Drop me off first, will you, Belle?"

"I'm dropping you off at our place, and that's where you will stay. Don't argue, my friend. Seeing the shape you're in, I can lick you myself if you do."

"No argument," Will said wearily.

At the house, Belle and the hack driver, one on either side of Will holding his arms, helped him up onto the porch steps. Belle guided him inside and over to the sofa in the living room.

"Lie down and stretch out, Will."

Will did so, and Belle lifted his feet onto the sofa and looked down at him. His eyes were closed, and she had the feeling that he was already more than half asleep.

She went out on the porch where the hack driver was waiting and said to him, "You're not through. Can you get a friend to help me move a bed downstairs?"

"Easy enough," he answered.

"Then I'll expect you later," Belle said.

21

From the GRANITE FORKS HERALD:

REVENGE TRY BRINGS DEATH

For three years Tom Riordan waited for revenge on Will Christie, deputy state marshal and secretary to the Lieutenant Governor, Joe Isom. Christie was a participant in the famous Tres Piedras shootout in which Riordan's older brother Hugh was killed. Tuesday morning before daylight on the porch of the Mineral City Hotel in Twin Buttes, Tom Riordan with two accomplices waited in ambush to even the score with Christie . . .

Brady Cope, on his way from the committee hearings, had bought the *Herald* from the newsboy hawking it in the Capitol corridor. He had moved to a window, read the opening paragraph of the story and did not bother to read the rest, because he already knew what it said.

Reaching the ground floor, he passed his own locked office and went on to the office of Joe Isom. The anteroom door was open but the room was empty. The door to Isom's office was ajar. He knocked on the doorframe, went in and saw that Joe was seated at his desk reading the *Herald*. Joe looked up at his entrance, tossed the paper on his desk and leaned back in his chair. As Brady took his customary seat Joe said, "Why did Riordan wait so long?"

"I suppose he'd been reading the *Herald* about Will's and Kevin's inspection trip. Here was a chance to catch him away from the Capitol. Can you think of another reason?"

"That's good enough. How was Will this morning?"

"Belle said better, although God knows he looked bad enough last night, didn't he?"

The evening before, Brady and Joe had heard Will's story in the library of the Evans house, where Will's bed had been put in order to be handy for Belle. They had talked with Will and had learned of his discovery of the Evans files at the CH. Neither of them had thought about much else this morning.

Now Brady said, "I missed dinner today to do some reading between the committee sessions. I don't think we have a leg to stand on, Joe, with a search warrant to recover those files. In the first place, Hatcher would refuse to honor the warrant. I'd have to send a small army down there to enforce the service. In the second place, he'd be right in refusing to turn over the files."

"Because they are Evans' personal files?"

Brady nodded. "We can't argue otherwise, because we don't know what's in the files. We don't know they contain any documents relating to the duties of the Attorney General's office."

"They were removed by fraud," Joe said.

"Fraud or not, they were Hugh's personal papers and belong to his estate. Something else I checked on:

Frank Jackson has been named executor of Hugh's estate. He showed the court a letter from Mrs. Evans naming him. Jackson probably telegraphed her to send the letter."

Brady rose, and Joe asked, "How'd it go in the committee hearings today?"

"It couldn't have gone worse," Brady replied. "Both sides see a chance to appoint five of their men to the Mining Commission. Both of those sets of men will have five mining inspectors. That'll be twenty well-paid jobs going to friends and relatives. All I can do is defend the statute, and it wasn't a good one to begin with."

"So it goes," Joe said.

Brady left for his own office, and now Joe, although he had read Lennie Piersall's story once, read it again. He'd never paid much attention to the names of the identified dead because he'd been too sick to care. By the time he was up and around again, it was ancient history. Still, the sheriff in Twin Buttes or Costigan must have identified the two Riordans as brothers. Joe still didn't understand why Tom Riordan had waited three years to make his move.

He thought back on Will's halting account last night of his visit to the CH and the discovery of Hugh Evans' files. Brady was right in saying they had no proof that the files contained papers relating to the Attorney General's office. And the first legal move Brady made to obtain the files, they would surely disappear and be hidden somewhere else.

Joe now recalled the State House gossip of last week that had turned out to be fact. Frank Jackson had been elected state chairman of the party. In this capacity he could legally take possession of Evans' files.

Joe rose, picked up his cane and, in spite of the discomfort, began a restless pacing of his office. There had to be a way to get those files out of Hatcher's place, short of starting a vicious and prolonged legal battle.

116

He halted abruptly. If Hatcher could be decoyed away from the CH there might be a chance of deceiving or bluffing Hatcher's men into releasing the files.

He went back to his desk and sat down, found pen and paper and began to write.

Jim Cousins and the horses arrived in Granite Forks around dark. He dropped the two extra horses at the feed stable. Since he had switched horses in mid-afternoon Will's horse was still comparatively fresh. As the hostler, a friend of Jim's, opened the gate to let the horses in, he called, "There's a note for you on the desk inside, Jim."

Jim dismounted and went into the tiny office, where the lamp was already lit. He recognized Brady's writing on the envelope. The note read: "Jim. Get some supper and then come on up to the house."

Jim was hungry, but in a way he didn't exactly understand he thought he detected a note of urgency in the words the note contained. He went out, mounted and headed upstreet for Cope's house, which he had visited once before to deliver a note to Belle from her father.

Lamps were lit in the house and he saw a horse tied to the hitching post out front. With barely a glance he identified it as Joe Isom's bay.

Brady answered the door and said, "Come in, Jim. Glad you're back."

And Jim, removing his hat, stepped into the room saying, "It was a nice ride. I'd like to do that oftener."

In the living room Belle was seated in an easy chair facing the sofa on which Joe and Will Christie sat. Jim said his good evenings and then looked at Will.

"You've got two eyes open, Will."

Will smiled and said, "I've decided I'm not coming apart, Jim."

Jim noticed several pieces of paper lying on the sofa between Will and Joe, and then he heard Brady say, "Sit down, Jim." Cope went over to a smaller easy

117

chair beside the table holding a lamp, and brought it over next to Jim and sat down.

"Have you eaten, Jim?" Belle asked.

"Yes, ma'am," Jim lied.

Belle knew he was lying, and she rose and said, "You wouldn't mind a cup of coffee, would you? I don't think any of us would." She went through the dining room into the kitchen.

Brady said now, "Jim, remember my telling you about the files that were stolen from our office?" At Jim's nod, he went on, "Will found 'em. They're at Clay Hatcher's CH ranch ten miles east of Twin Buttes. Show him the layout, Will. Jim, take Belle's chair under the lamp."

As Will extended the paper he said, "I'll be going down with you, Jim, but I can't go with you to the CH. They damn well know me, and would hold me for Hatcher. You're a new face down there."

Jim went over to take a sheet of paper Will held out, then sat down in Belle's chair. From memory, then, Will described the big-house layout, while Jim followed it on the map. Will went on to tell him of the first meeting with Hatcher, and of his dismissal.

"Those dotted lines you see show where I walked while I waited to see His Majesty. I marked the location of the files in Hatcher's bedroom."

Jim studied the map in silence, then looked up at Will. "I just go ask for them," he said.

Will and Joe laughed; Brady smiled, and so did Jim.

"Take over, Joe," Brady said.

Joe picked up another sheet of paper and held it out to Jim.

"Tonight after you leave here, we want you to take this telegram to the night operator at the depot. Read it, please."

Jim sat down and read the telegram It said:

CLAY HATCHER
CH RANCH
TWIN BUTTES

IN FAIRNESS TO YOUR INTERESTS IN THE MARY E I URGE YOU TO APPEAR IN PERSON BEFORE THE CONFERENCE COMMITTEE HEARINGS ON THE CREATION OF A NEW MINING COMMISSION STOP YOUR REPRESENTATIVE HERE HAS REFUSED TO TESTIFY ON RIGHTS GRANTED BY THE 5TH AMENDMENT STOP AS ATTORNEY GENERAL I OPPOSE THE BILL CREATING A NEW MINING COMMISSION BUT I THINK IT ONLY JUST THAT YOUR VIEWS AS ONE OF THE LARGEST MINE OWNERS IN THE STATE SHOULD BE HEARD STOP SINCE THE LIST OF WITNESSES IS COMING TO AN END I AGAIN URGE YOU TO APPEAR HERE AT YOUR EARLIEST CONVENIENCE STOP ON WORD FROM YOU I WILL SCHEDULE YOUR TESTIMONY WITH THE CONFERENCE COMMITTEE CHAIRMAN FULL STOP CORDIALLY BRADY COPE ATTORNEY GENERAL

Jim thought a moment, then said, "This is to get Hatcher away from the place, I take it."

Joe nodded and picked up another sheet of paper and held it out. Jim took it, sat down and read it. It said:

Dear Clay,

As you know I was elected chairman of the party last week. I don't much like the chore but I think I may be of some service to our friends.

I find I am very much in need of Hugh Evans' files which I stored with you some weeks ago. To save you the trouble of sending a man to deliver and guard the files, I am sending a trusted young friend down there to pick them up. He is the bearer of this letter and his name is Jim Cousins. Any assistance you and your men can give him will be greatly appreciated.

The hearings on the new Mining Commission bill are nearly finished. The Conference Committee, as a whole, seems overwhelmingly in favor of its passage. My informed count shows 20 in favor, with 2 opposed. Even with the inevitable few last-minute switches, we will have a solid majority of the Committee in favor of the new bill.

I'd go into more details only Jim's waiting to catch

the train, so forgive this last minute note. My thanks and kindest regards.

Cordially
Frank
—*Frank E. Jackson*

FEJ/jc

"Why is the single 'Frank' written in different-colored ink?" Jim asked.

"He dictated the letter to a secretary, read it, then signed it with his own pen and ink after reading it."

"Why the 'Frank E. Jackson' below the 'Frank'? It's in the secretary's handwriting."

"That's to identify him to Hatcher's foreman," Joe said. "The single 'Frank' wouldn't mean a thing."

"Is that the way he really writes 'Frank'—with the capital F not connected with the r?"

Joe reached in his hip pocket, brought out his wallet, extracted a card from it and held it out to Jim, saying, "The Lieutenant Governor along with the Governor gets a pass from the Rocky Mountain Central. Here it is, and this is Frank's signature."

Jim compared the "Frank" on the pass with that of the letter, then handed the pass back to Joe.

"They sure look alike," he said.

Belle came in then with coffee and passed the cups around.

Brady patted the seat of the easy chair and said, "Sit here, Belle. Jim needed some light."

Jim's saucer held a sandwich and when he tasted the coffee he knew that Belle had put whiskey in it. She was watching him and he smiled his thanks.

"Any other questions, Jim?" Brady asked.

"Yes. How did you come by this stationery with the Rocky Mountain Central letterhead?"

"It was in my desk," Brady said. "Hugh was attorney for the railroad."

Jim grinned. "All right, say I can get the files, then what?"

Will was first off the train at Twin Buttes. He stepped onto the lamp-lit platform and turned right, passing by the night agent, who was already talking to the brakeman. They both looked at him and his bandaged head as he passed.

After two other passengers had descended to the platform, Jim Cousins followed. He did not even look in Will's direction, but turned left skirting the depot, and headed for the Mineral City Hotel. As he rounded the corner he saw Will shoulder open the batwing doors of the Bullseye and disappear inside.

At the hotel, Jim registered at the desk and was given a key to a second-floor room. Inside it he lit the lamp, threw his blanketroll on the chair, undressed and climbed into bed. He did not think anyone who had seen him since he and Will got on the train in Granite Forks had associated the two of them. They had taken separate seats and not spoken with each other, and had gone different ways at the depot. It was important that they not be connected, because Will could be identified here and his actions observed and reported. After reviewing his instructions for tomorrow, Jim slept.

Next morning he carried his blanketroll downstairs, threw it in a corner behind the desk, and was first in the dining room. Will had not shown up when he had finished.

He retrieved his blanketroll, shouldered it, tapped

his hip pocket to make sure he had the letter to Hatcher in it, then headed for the depot. He found the agent out sweeping the platform with a wide pushbroom. The agent saw him approach and stopped sweeping.

Jim said, "Morning. I got a letter for Mr. Clay Hatcher. How do I find him?"

The agent looked him over, smiled faintly and said, "You don't. He took the train to Granite Forks yesterday afternoon."

"Hell," Jim said in disgust. "Know when he'll be back?"

The agent shook his head. "He don't tell me those things."

Jim said, "I can wait. Thanks." He headed for the feed stable.

He found the owner in the small office, a spry, white-haired, tobacco-chewing man. He was talking to another man, who was roughly dressed and had an expressionless pock-marked, unshaven face.

Jim stated his needs after throwing his blanketroll in the corner. He wanted to hire a team and a wagon for two days. He wanted a man to accompany him. He wanted a ration of oats for the team. Could the stable owner accommodate him?

The old man had ceased his chewing as he listened to Jim's wants. Now he spat into a foul-looking spittoon beside him and said, "All that'll take money. You got it?"

Jim reached in his hip pocket, drew out a small buckskin poke and asked, "How much? I'll pay you when I pick up the wagon."

The old man had already made his calculations. "Twenty-five dollars. That includes the wage for the man I send with you."

Jim untied his poke, shook out an eagle and a double eagle, and held them in his hand so the old man could see them.

When the old man recovered from his surprise, he said, "Well, come 'round about noon."

"No," Jim said flatly. "I'll be back in half an hour.

I can hitch up a team in fifteen minutes; so can your hostler."

"All right," the old man said humbly.

"Now, show me your wagons. I want the smallest one you've got."

Jim put the coins back in the buckskin. The old man rose and Jim followed him through the runway and out into the back lot. The long, open-faced wagonshed held half a dozen buggies, a couple of buckboards and some wagons. He chose a small wagon with a water key ironed to its sideboard.

Back at the hotel he went to the dining-room door, saw Will seated at a table at the far end, made sure Will saw him, and then went up to his room. Within minutes there was a soft knock on his door and Will stepped in, closing the door behind him.

"Hatcher left yesterday afternoon," Jim said. "I'm picking up a wagon and a helper in half an hour. I took it for two days just so Magruder wouldn't be looking for me tonight."

Will smiled and said, "You'd leave too if the Attorney General called you in. The two days is a good idea." He rubbed his hands together in mock avarice, "We're in business, Jim. Now describe to me the files."

"Iron bar running through the drawer handles, ironed to the top, and two padlocks."

Will nodded, and Jim noticed now that the swelling in his face was nearly gone, although the bruise marks still showed.

"Well, I'm off to see Kevin," Will said. "I'll pick you up at the turnover. There's a tank down the turnoff road so we'll have water for the horses. Know who your helper will be?"

"No idea, Will."

"You're not carrying a gun and you've got money on you, so watch him."

At Jim's nod, he said, "Good luck, my friend. I'll see you later."

After Will left, Jim decided he might as well leave too. His presence at the stables might hurry up the hostler. He waited only a few minutes to let Will clear the building, and then went down into the lobby. After paying his bill he backtracked to the feed stable. Looking through the runway, he saw the hostler and another man finishing up hitching the team.

He went into the office, where the old man was seated at the desk and gave him a double eagle and an eagle, in return for which the old man gave him five silver dollars.

The old man's curiosity, which Jim had anticipated, finally surfaced.

"You loadin' here?"

"Yes," Jim said. "I'll see you day after tomorrow."

When Jim picked up his blanketroll and went out to the harnessed team, the wagon was hitched and both the hostler and the other man were filling buckets from the pipe running into the horse trough and emptying them into the wooden keg. The hostler paused to say, "This here's Red Sterns, mister. He's going with you."

Jim nodded, and Red gave him a nod in reply.

In a minute the water keg was capped, and Jim and Red climbed up on the seat and the hostler handed Jim the reins.

Jim turned the team right when he hit the street, went a block, turned right again, went up two blocks, took another right and when he hit the main road he turned left.

Red, a work-worn, gaunt man of thirty, could have been without speech, for he was absolutely silent for the first hour they drove. When they came in close sight of the mountains Jim asked, "Those the San Dimas?"

Red cleared his throat and said, "Dun'no. I'm new 'round here."

That was the extent of their conversation until Jim pulled the team up in front of the door of the cook shack at the CH, where a Mexican, canvas apron around his midriff, was lounging.

Jim called, "Where's your ramrod, *amigo?*"

124

The cook pointed with his chin and said, "Last door in the bunkhouse."

"What's his name?" Jim asked.

"Charles Turner."

Jim thanked him and moved the team ahead, pulling up before an open door. He handed the reins to Red and stepped down. He knocked on the door, heard a gruff voice tell him to come in, and stepped into a small office where a gaunt, weather-burned man in his late forties was seated before an ancient roll-top desk. At the sound of his footstep the foreman looked at him. He was, Jim guessed, a Texas transplant—brown, bleach-eyed and slow-moving.

"You Charlie Turner, Clay Hatcher's forman?"

At the man's nod Jim reached in his pocket, drew out the envelope and said, "I'm Jim Cousins. I got a letter here for Mr. Hatcher."

"Mr. Hatcher ain't here. He's in Granite Forks."

"I found that out in town," Jim said pleasantly. "Mr. Jackson told me if Mr. Hatcher wasn't here you should open his letter and read it."

Jim moved over to the desk and held out the letter, which Turner took. He looked at the name on the corner of the envelope.

"Oh, Frank Jackson. He was out here a few weeks back. How is he?"

"Just like always," Jim said.

Turner opened the envelope, got out of his chair, moved over to the closest window and unfolded the letter. He read it slowly and carefully, then came over and extended his hand. "Glad to meet you, Jim. I know what Frank's written about. I helped lug that file in."

Charlie Turner then went back to his desk and from a drawer took a ring of keys.

He led the way out of the door, and when he saw the wagon he called up to Red, "Follow us."

He and Jim headed for the patio door in the south wall.

"What kind of work do you do for Frank, Jim?"

Jim thought quickly, then answered, "Oh, things like

125

this. Both Frank's secretaries are getting too old to travel. On weekends, when they don't work, I guess you could call me Frank's sorry substitute secretary."

"Like the job?"

"I like the man, but not the job," Jim answered.

This brought a smile from Charlie. Jim made a mental note to look in the next mirror he came upon to see if his teeth had turned black from this lie.

They halted at the open double door in the wall, let the wagon catch up with them and then Jim called, "Come along, Red."

Red climbed down, and wound the reins around a wagon wheel. The three of them went through the door and turned left, heading for the blue door that Will had described to him. Before they reached the door, however, Charlie turned right, moved up to the next door, halted, isolated a key from the several on the ring, and opened the door.

It was hot in this close room. Charlie moved toward the wardrobe, Jim and Red following him. He halted, pointed to the barred file cabinet and said, "That's what you're after, Jim."

"Grab it by the top and tilt it toward you, Red. I'll take the bottom," Jim said.

Red went over to the cabinet, walked it out from the wall and tilted it. He gave Jim an inquiring look, which Jim didn't see. Jim moved over now, knelt, grasped the base of the file cabinet and lifted it off the floor. He looked at Charlie. "Come here, Charlie, and heft this."

Charlie, a look of puzzlement on his face, came over and took Jim's place, a hand on either side of the cabinet. He lifted it twice up to his chest, then looked at Jim.

"Hell, it's empty." He put it down and said to Red, "Straighten it up, Red."

Red did so, and now Charlie examined the two padlocks on the top of the cabinet. They were both open. He slipped them from their hasps, slid the rod out from the drawer pulls, then, holding the rod in one hand, he pulled all four drawers of the cabinet open. All were empty.

Jim looked at Charlie and said, "I don't think Frank sent me out here for an empty file. He could get one in town."

Charlie leaned the bar against the wardrobe, walked past it, turned left into a short passageway and opened the door into Hatcher's office-library. He walked into the middle of the room and halted. Jim came up and stopped beside him. They were both looking at the red sofa on which were a dozen high stacks of papers.

"What was supposed to be in that there file, Jim?"

"Frank didn't say."

Charlie frowned and said, "Hell, I can't give you anything from Mr. Hatcher's office, especially when I don't know what I'm looking for."

"Try something, Charlie," Jim said. He gestured toward the stacks of paper on the sofa. "You go through a bunch of those papers. See who those letters are addressed to. It doesn't matter who signed them. Don't tell me the name of the man they're addressed to. After you've looked at 'em, I think I can tell you."

Charlie looked at him with a puzzled and suspicious expression. "I don't think Mr. Hatcher would like me lookin' at his letters."

"You won't be reading any of them," Jim pointed out. "Just see who they're addressed to."

Almost reluctantly Charlie moved over to the sofa, sat on the low table and started on the nearest pile of letters. He went through a dozen on the first pile, then shifted to the second pile. After looking at half a dozen there he moved on to the others, sampling some letters from each.

Then he turned and looked at Jim. "All right. You tell me his name."

"They're all addressed to Hugh B. Evans, Attorney General," Jim said.

A look of astonishment came over Charlie's face; it vanished quickly, to be replaced by an expression of fierce suspicion. Charlie rose and moved over in front of Jim.

"I thought you said Jackson never told you what was in the cabinet?"

"He didn't have to," Jim said. "Did you read or hear that Frank Jackson was just elected state chairman of the party?"

"What if I did?" Charlie asked in a truculent tone of voice.

"Well, Hugh B. Evans was chairman before Frank. He died a few weeks ago." Jim gestured toward the papers. "My guess is those are Evans' party files. Political stuff."

"What are they doing out here?"

Jim shrugged. "I don't know, Charlie, but I can sure make a guess."

Charlie waited, watching him.

Jim went on. "Frank and Mr. Hatcher have been close friends for a long time. You know that. My guess is that Frank could use your boss's advice on a lot of things happening in the state. I reckon Frank sent out these things so Mr. Hatcher could get a background so he could help Frank."

"That makes sense," Charlie said deliberately. He thought a minute. "What if Mr. Hatcher ain't through reading 'em?"

"Well, your boss is in Granite Forks now. I can have those files in Frank's office tomorrow evening. He can read them there."

Charlie reflected on this, and then said almost mournfully, "I sure would admire it if you could wait until Mr. Hatcher gets back."

"Make sense, Charlie," Jim prodded. "What's the difference if he reads them here or in Frank's office?"

"Well, I reckon you're right," Charlie said reluctantly. He turned to Red. "Go lug the file cabinet in here, Red. We'll pack this stuff up."

Red disappeared into the bedroom and returned carrying the file case and the steel locking rod.

"We'll do this, Red," Jim said. "You go water the team."

When Red was gone Jim pulled out the top drawer from the file cabinet, set it on the low table and, beginning with the closest stack of letters, he put them face down in the drawer.

Charlie watched him, and Jim was careful to demonstrate that with the letters face down he could not have read a single line while he was packing them. When he had one drawer full he slipped it into the file cabinet, and now Charlie took a drawer and worked along beside him. The last drawer was only half full when they had cleared off the red sofa.

Jim felt a quiet elation as he picked up the locking rod, slipped it through the drawer pulls, removed the two padlocks from their hasps, let the rod settle and secured it with the padlocks, which he left open.

Charlie watched him glumly, and when Jim had finished Charlie looked at him and shook his head.

"I dun'no, Jim. I can catch hell for this."

"Don't worry about it, Charlie. If you can find some paper I'll sign a receipt for the files. I got my blanket-roll in the wagon. I'll put those files in the baggage room in the depot. I'll sleep beside it. After the agent locks me in I'll stick by 'em tomorrow until the train goes." He shook his head and smiled faintly. "I don't want to lose 'em any more than you do."

Charlie nodded, went over to Clay Hatcher's desk and searched the drawers until he found some paper, then turned and said, "Make out your receipt, Jim."

Jim moved over to the desk, took up a pen, flipped up the cover of the inkwell, sat down and wrote out a receipt.

While he was writing, Red came back into the room. When Jim was finished he gave the receipt to Charlie, who read it, folded it and put it in his shirt pocket, saying, "Might as well take it out through the bedroom."

It was a hefty load even for Jim and Red. They moved the cabinet out into the patio and headed for the wagon while Charlie locked the bedroom door.

Once the cabinet was in the wagonbed and covered by Jim's blankets, Jim turned to face Charlie and held out his hand.

"I'll likely be seeing you around somewhere, Charlie. Thanks for the help. I'll tell Frank how you found the stuff."

They shook hands, and as Jim walked around the end of the wagon he double-checked the tail gate. Red unwound the reins and handed them to Jim, who slacked the team into motion. The horses made a tight half-circle and headed out for the main road.

Jim was drenched with sweat, and it was not from moving the file cabinet. *That was a real close one,* he reflected. He didn't know what would happen to Charlie when Clay Hatcher learned of what Charlie had done. He didn't much care either. It might be a good idea for him to keep a gun in his desk from now on. If Charlie ever learned who he was, he just might ask for time off to go to the State House and even the score.

He was startled when Red spoke. "Big outfit, huh?"

"Yeah, big outfit," Jim agreed.

There was no more talk until they were out of the foothill country. The sun, Jim noticed, was almost overhead, which gave them a good four hours to make the railroad.

About a half-hour later Jim came to a turnoff road and saw Will lounging in the thin shade of a big mequite. His livery horse was tied in the shade of a tree close by.

As Jim reined the team to a halt, Will untied his horse and led it over.

Will first looked in the wagonbed, saw the files and grinned up at Jim. "Found something along the way, huh?"

Jim nodded. "Yeah. The horses stumbled over it."

Will untied a packed flour sack from his saddle and said to Jim, "Ask your partner if he'll ride my horse," and walked around the back of the wagon, untying the sack. Red climbed down and Will faced him. He reached in the sack, brought out a loaf of bread, broke off a big chunk and handed it to Red. Then he fished out some jerky from the sack and gave it to him.

"Eat up," Will said. Red nodded his thanks and Will climbed up into the seat.

"How's Kevin?" Jim asked first.

"Bad, very bad," Will said soberly. "Doc Kelly's going to have to take his leg off."

"Can he do it?"

Will said, "He says so. He was a contract surgeon for the army. He says he's done plenty of 'em." He looked at Jim now and asked, "Any reason you can't go on alone from Millerton to home?"

"No reason at all. Why?"

"I thought I'd go back so I could be with Kevin. He'll be one lonely old boy at a time like this."

"Good idea, do it," Jim said. "I can find my way to Millerton by myself. You could go back now."

"No, that's why I came along," Will said. "If you don't know the country you could wander around in it for a week. Doc Kelly said he'd wait until I got back there."

Jim nodded at Will. "Looks like he worked on you too. Where's your bandage?"

"I threw it away," Will said.

"What about your nose?"

"I threw the splints away too. Now tell me what happened at the CH."

Jim gave the account of his recovery of the files. Will listened to the story of the argument with Charlie Turner with deep pleasure. Charlie had been outbluffed by Kevin, and now by Jim. If what he had seen of Clay Hatcher's temper was any example, Charlie would very likely soon be riding the grub line.

They ate then, and when they had finished Will said, "Hand over the reins, Jim. It's about time I earned my money."

Jim gave him the reins and it wasn't long before he was glad he had. About half a dozen roads from small mines in the area joined the rough road they were traveling, some of them more heavily traveled than

131

this one. At last, Will turned the team left to a road that wasn't even a road, but only a track.

Some of the time Jim thought that Will was really bushwhacking in this gully-slashed, arid country.

When Jim was sure they were lost he didn't say so. Instead he asked, "How come you know this country so well?"

"Before I was brand inspector, I was chairman for a survey crew. We mapped this stretch for the railroad."

They stopped once to water the team, and then pressed on into mid-afternoon. Red, on Will's horse, held his position to one side of them to escape the plume of dust trailing the wagon. Presently, in the distance, almost obscured by mesquites, Jim saw a high sun-bleached water tank which, because of its shape and height, could belong only to the railroad. Minutes later they broke out of the mesquite and picked up a well-traveled road coming in from the northeast. Above them to the right was the water tank, and across the tracks a fair-sized adobe building with weather-scarred frame outbuildings.

"Well, this is Millerton," Will said. "Population three, and a flagstop on the Rocky Mountain Central."

He pulled the team off the road and halted it midway between the water tank and the road, opposite the adobe building across the tracks.

"Might as well leave the files in the wagon. It'll be easier to load it from there than from the ground," he said. He handed the reins to Jim. "I'll go get the flag from old man Miller."

He climbed down, crossed the tracks and approached the open door of the adobe building. The room he entered had the appearance of a sparsely stocked general store. Asleep on the counter to his right, his head pillowed on a pile of saddle blankets, was a stocky, grey-haired old man who opened his eyes at the sound of Will's footsteps.

Will said, "Don't get up, Mr. Miller. How are you?"

He walked over to the man and extended his hand,

saying, "Remember me? I used to work on the survey crew."

The old man, still lying down, shook hands with Will.

"Will . . . Will . . . Will . . . something."

"Christie," Will answered.

"That's right. What are you doing here?"

"I'm about to flag the train, if I can borrow your flag."

Mr. Miller pointed with his thumb to a shelf behind the counter. Will looked and saw the furled red flag wedged between the shelf partition and some bolts of dress goods. He went around the counter, picked up the flag and said, "How are things going?"

"Just the same," Miller said wearily.

"I got one piece of freight I want to take with me. Who do I pay?"

"The brakeman. He'll keep the money, too."

"All right. Go back to sleep," Will said.

When he stepped out, he could hear the sound of the train in the distance.

He crossed the tracks and when the train was in sight he unfurled the flag, waited a minute, then waved it, stood beside the tracks and waited. The train, hissing as it slowed down, applied its brakes, coasted past Will and came to a panting halt.

The door of the baggage car was open, and now Jim maneuvered the wagon until he was even with the doors.

The baggage man watched as Will and Jim loaded the file cabinet into the car and laid it on its back. Will straightened up and said, "Brady and Joe are meeting you at the depot. Get a hack driver to help you unload. Tell Joe when you see him where I am and why. He'll understand."

Jim nodded. "Tell Kevin I wish him the best of luck. God knows he'll need it."

Will lowered himself to the wagonbed and climbed down from the wagon. The baggage man signaled the engineer and the train slowly got under way for Granite Forks.

When the train was past and he didn't have to talk above its clatter, Will said to Red, "Take the team back to the feed stable, Red. You better pick up the tracks we made. You paid up?"

Red nodded.

"Then I'll see you around," Will said.

He picked up the flag from the wagonbed, mounted his horse, crossed the tracks and left the flag at Miller's. Then he watered his horse at Miller's corral parallel with the tracks.

23

Will arrived just before dark and headed straight for Doc Kelly's house. The lamp in the waiting room was already lit, and the door to the office was ajar.

"Doc, it's me," Will called out.

The door opened and the doctor came into the waiting room. He held a bottle of whiskey by its neck in one hand; the other held two glasses.

"How's Kevin?" Will asked.

The doctor moved over to the table that held the lamp, poured a drink in one glass and freshened his own. He walked over to Will, gestured to a chair and said, "Sit down, Will."

Will took the drink, sat down and repeated his question. "How's Kevin, Doc?"

Doctor Kelly turned his drink-flushed face to Will and said quietly, "He's dead."

Will was silent for stunned moments, trying to accept this. He knew Kevin had been in danger, but not near death. Will saw that the doctor was half drunk and the thought that crossed his mind he put into words.

"Did you take off his leg, Doc?"

"No. I told you I'd wait for you. I didn't touch him." He went over and sat down and took a drink.

"What killed him?"

"From the look of his face I'd judge a stroke of apoplexy. I came back from a couple of early afternoon calls and looked in on him the first thing. He'd died while I was out. I couldn't have helped him if I'd been here, Will."

"Can I see him?"

"They've taken him. They have to do that when it's as hot as it is."

Will nodded and looked at his drink, feeling a wild rage churning inside him. How senseless and unnecessary Kevin's death was. He had been hurt and had died because some idiot wanted to even an old score that had never involved Kevin.

Will drank from his glass, his hand so shaking with his anger that the glass rattled against his teeth. He swallowed the fiery whiskey and softly said, "God damn it."

"Yes," Doc Kelly said. "He was a fine old boy. I wish I'd known him better."

Will sat motionless, lost in thought. There had to be a way to find the man responsible for Kevin's death. He thought back on the story in the *Herald* about the attack on them. Riordan had been riding a newly bought horse branded WW. *Anybody working on that,* he wondered.

He came to his decision, finished his drink, rose and said, "I owe you money, Doc."

"Not a red cent," the doctor said. "I liked him."

"I did too," Will agreed bitterly. "I liked him so much I'm going to find out who killed him."

Doc looked at him curiously. "How?"

"I don't know, Doc. Riordan had a bill of sale for a horse. The brand on it must be registered. I'll take it from there. Who's the brand inspector here?"

"Bill Sales. He lives on the far side of the Catholic church."

"Kevin told me he had no family. I reckon that means he'll be buried here." At Doc Kelly's nod Will said, "Who do I see about paying for the burial?"

"Stop by the hardware store tomorrow and ask for Al Woodson."

"I'll be gone. Have him send his bill to me at the State Capitol building," Will said.

Will held out his hand. "I'll be in touch with you, Doc. Thank you for everything."

They shook hands and Will went out.

He mounted and headed for Main Street and the Catholic church. He wondered why he had waited for so long before getting on the trail of the man responsible for Kevin's death. He knew the answer to that question without having to speculate. While Kevin was only seriously hurt it was up to Deputy Sheriff Thompson to investigate. But if the fugitives had fled to another county then it would be out of Thompson's jurisdiction. All he could do was write the sheriffs of the surrounding counties and ask them to search for two whose names he couldn't give them and ask that they be returned here. With so little information to go on it was unlikely that any of the sheriffs would put out much effort in search for the two men. But now with Kevin dead it was murder, murder of his friend, and a killer to be tracked down.

The house on the east side of the Catholic church was a small frame building, and lamps lit up the ground-floor windows. Will climbed the steps of the porch and knocked on the door. It was answered by a slight, wiry man of middle age dressed in range clothes.

"Mr. Sales?" Will asked.

When the man acknowledged that he was Sales, Will said, "I understand you're the brand inspector here. I used to be one myself. I'm surprised I found you home."

The man laughed. "You don't very often. What's on you mind, Mr.—?"

"Christie," Will said. They shook hands. "I'd like to look at your brand-registration book. I'm trying to track down the owner and location of the WW brand."

"You don't have to look at the book," Sales said. "Sheriff Thompson asked me all this yesterday. It's a horse ranch just outside Hidalgo. That's down south in Higbee County. Owner's name is Bill Wilcox."

"Hidalgo is on the Rocky Mountain Central, isn't it?"

"Yes, sir, end of the line."

"Much obliged to you for your information, Mr. Sales. I'm only sorry I had to call at suppertime."

They said good-bye and Will went out to his horse, mounted and headed for the feed stable. In reviewing what Sales had just said, it abruptly came to him that the southbound train was due shortly in Twin Buttes. He could catch the night train south. That, he was certain, Kevin would have approved of.

He lifted his horse into a trot, stopped at the hotel, paid his bill, got his warbag and dropped his horse at the feed stable. While he was waiting for change he heard the whistle of the train coming from the north.

Making the short distance to the depot, he bought a ticket from the harried night agent, who wrote out a ticket and then hurried out to the platform to trundle his baggage cart to the far end of the platform. The other passengers were on the platform waiting for the train, whose headlamp Will could see when he was through the door.

24

When the train slowly pulled up to the depot platform in Granite Forks, both Jim and the baggage master stood in the open door of the baggage car. As the car coasted past the waiting passengers, Jim saw both Brady and Joe leaning against the station wall. Jim waved and Brady waved back, while Joe spoke to two husky men beside him who started immediately for the baggage car.

When the train halted the two men approached and stopped at the door. Jim slid the file case toward them and patted it, saying, "This side up." The two men took it and Jim vaulted to the platform and moved toward Brady and Joe.

Approaching him, Brady said, "Is what's under that blanket what I think it is?"

Jim grinned. "Yes, sir."

They shook hands, and then Jim shook hands with Joe.

"That calls for a very tall drink. We'll have it in a few minutes, Jim." Joe looked at the car, "Where's Will?"

"He stayed over. I'll tell you about that later."

The three of them went around the depot, where a hack and a team and a wagon were waiting.

They paused beside the hack, watching the men load the file case into the wagon.

Jim said then, "I brought it this far. I reckon I'll ride with it to the end of the line."

He climbed into the wagon and sat on the file cabinet, while Joe and Brady stepped into the hack, which was driven ahead of the wagon.

At the Evans house Brady and Joe went ahead. Brady held the door open while the two workmen carried the cabinet in. They set it down in the middle of the living room, and Brady was paying them off when Jim stepped into the room.

As the two men left, Belle came in from the kitchen, gave Jim a warm greeting and then said to her father, "You have time for just one drink before supper, Pa."

Her glance lifted to Jim and she said, "Jim, don't you tell a word about your trip until we're all at the table."

She and Brady went back into the kitchen then to fix drinks. Joe limped over to the file cabinet standing in the middle of the room, pulled off the blanket, folded it and tossed it on a chair, afterwards coming back to the sofa where Jim was sitting.

"What about Will? Is he all right?" Joe asked.

Jim said he was, but Kevin wasn't. He was going to lose a leg, so Will had gone back to Twin Buttes from Millerton to be with him. Jim finished by saying, "Will said you would understand." Joe only nodded. His sober, homely face showed a sudden sadness. He, more than anyone else, knew what Kevin was going through, for he had come very close to losing his leg too. He'd been lucky and Kevin wasn't.

When the drinks came Jim asked if he could wash up and Belle showed him to the back porch, where a bucket of water and a basin stood on a bench, a clean towel hanging above.

Jim took a slug of his drink, set the glass on the bench, stripped off his shirt and washed off the desert dust from his body and face. Afterwards he beat his shirt against the wall to rid it of the dust before he put it back on.

As soon as he stepped into the living room Jim knew that Joe had told Brady and Belle about Kevin. Jim

139

sat down with his drink and Belle asked, "Did you see Kevin at all, Jim?"

Jim said he hadn't, for he and Will couldn't be seen together, and he told them that he had hired a team and a handyman and was headed for the CH while Will looked in on Kevin.

When their drinks were finished Belle called them to the table and brought the food. After they were served Belle said, "We left you on your way to the CH, Jim. What happened there?"

Jim recounted then his meeting with Charlie Turner and told of Turner's ready acceptance of the forged letter. He described to them his dismay when they discovered the files were empty. His account of his argument with Turner and his own identification of the file papers by naming Hugh Evans as the recipient of all the papers brought a smile from all of them, and a proud one from Brady. Anyone who could think on his feet that fast had the makings of a good lawyer, Brady decided. The rest of Jim's story, telling of meeting Will and driving to Millerton, was brief.

All of them helped Belle carry out the dishes. Afterwards, back in the living room, Brady walked over to the file cabinet, leaned an arm on it and said, "Belle, we're going to make a mess around here, but it can't be helped. You heard Jim say that he and Turner simply shoved Hugh's correspondence into the files at random."

He went on to explain what he proposed to do to save hours, even days, of sifting through Hugh Evans' correspondence. He proposed that this evening all of them divide up the files between them. They would pile them on the dining-room table to sort them alphabetically according to the name of the sender. When finished, they would go through the individual letters, which would be then read aloud so the significance of the letters could be judged and the unimportant ones separated from the others.

Belle said, "I think you and Joe should be the judges

of their importance, Pa. You and Joe will know the men who wrote them. Jim and I won't."

This was agreed on, and Brady pulled out the first drawer, carried it into the dining room and invited them to help themselves.

They made relatively short work of the alphabetical sorting, after which they moved to more comfortable seats in the living room. Joe and Brady sat side by side on the sofa, and Jim handed them a stack and the real work began. By the time they were through the C's, under which companies were filed, Brady knew they had struck a mine of secret information. When they were finished with the E's, which contained Evans' replies to letters, they came to the truly damning evidence. These acknowledged receipts of cash, promises of favors and letters signed by Evans saying Governor Kilgore had instructed him to answer as party chairman.

By two o'clock when they finished they all realized they had in their possession the working, political guts and history of Sam Kilgore's party organization. When Belle came in from the kitchen a little after two, there were better than fifty letters stacked beside Joe. As Belle passed coffee around she looked closely at her father. His face was pale and at the same time excited, but his eyes seemed dazed.

Belle went back into the kitchen, picked up a bottle of whiskey and brought it back into the living room.

"Put some in your coffee, Pa. You look tired. We're all tired."

Brady and Joe helped themselves, Belle carried the bottle to Jim, and then she poured a tiny bit in her own cup of coffee and sat down.

"Well, Pa, how does it stand?" she asked.

Brady took a sip of his reinforced coffee, was quiet a moment, then said, "When this gets out, their machine will be wrecked. Old Sam will be totally destroyed." He looked at Jim, lifted his cup and said, "You just shot down a Governor."

25

Shortly after daylight the train whistle for Hidalgo brought Will to a sleep-drugged consciousness. During the near twelve-hour train ride he had gotten so used to the jolting, racking movement that he had managed to get several hours of sleep.

He sat up, reached for his gunbelt under the seat, rose and strapped it on and saw the brakeman walking toward him up the aisle. Will gave him a good morning and asked, "Any place for grub open this early?"

"There's a place next to the hotel. You can't miss it."

The brakeman passed him, calling, "Next stop Hidalgo. Everybody off. Next stop Hildalgo."

Will looked out the window and saw he was heading into a grey overcast day that held the promise of rain. He stretched now and felt a twinge in his ribcage that told him his ribs might be mending, but not this fast. The train began to slow down and the brakeman came past headed in the other direction. Will rubbed his face, felt the beard stubble and wondered when his next shave would happen along.

When the train stopped and he got off, he stepped down from the depot platform and saw the hotel and the café next to it.

After a big breakfast, with blanketroll over his shoulder he headed down past the hotel to the feed stable in the next block.

From what he could see of Hidalgo, it seemed almost a one street town, although it was the county seat. It was in high foothill country with sparse timber crowding to the edge of town. A small, two-story brown-painted building held a sign at a right angle over the boardwalk proclaiming, *Higbee County Courthouse,* and below it, *Masonic Hall Upstairs.*

The feed stable was a block beyond. Here Will hired a horse, left his warbag and borrowed a beat-up yellow slicker, tied it behind the cantle and then asked directions to the WW ranch.

He headed out east, crossed the tracks with the Central's roundhouse to his right and was on a well-traveled road.

Within an hour he was riding down the long lane leading to the big log house and big barns and stables of the WW ranch.

He passed the house under big cottonwoods and headed across the barn lot. He saw a sign on the end wall of the log bunkhouse. It bore the WW brand, below which was printed the word *Office* in big letters.

As Will headed for it, he noted the pastures off to his right where a couple of dozen mares with their colts were grazing. The winter feed was up and he saw several huge stacks circled by slat fences to protect them against the stock.

Will knew he had been seen when a man left a barn and moved toward the office. Will dismounted, tied his horse and observed the man approaching. He was a thin man in his thirties, so tall that Will knew he would have to look up to see his long, good-humored face. He did, when the man halted in front of him.

"I'm looking for Bill Wilcox," Will said.

"He's away on a trip," the puncher said. "Anything I can do for you?"

Will introduced himself and they shook hands as the puncher said, "Ray Sweet. I'm Wilcox's foreman."

"Then you'd likely know. A couple of weeks ago, or

around then, you sold a horse to a fellow named Tom Riordan. Do you remember it?"

Sweet snorted. "I ain't likely to forget it. Them three come in here so drunk I don't see how they stuck to their horses. Riordan wanted to buy a horse, and take it from me that's something. He never rode a horse he didn't borrow or steal. I was set to run 'em off when he showed me his money. Well, that's our business, so I sold him a bay gelding."

"You said 'them three.' There were two others with him?"

Sweet nodded, tilted his head and said, "Them two set against the wall drinkin' while Riordan and me rode out to look over some of our stuff. He liked this bay, but he was so damned drunk I had to switch his saddle for him."

They felt the first drops of rain and Sweet said, "Bring your horse over here," and started for an open-faced wagon shed a few yards from the office.

Will led his horse to shelter. Sweet was standing under the shed roof watching the rain and Will brought his horse in, wrapped the reins around a wagon wheel and joined him.

"We can sure use this," Sweet said.

Will agreed, then said, "About those two men with Riordan. Know who they were?"

"Everybody around here does," Sweet said in disgust. "They're just riffraff. If one McCartney ain't in jail, the other one is."

"Brothers?"

"Yep. Their ma ought to be ashamed of 'em, except she's dead. Maybe they're why she is."

"Know where I can find 'em?"

Sweet turned his head and looked at him. "Yep. You sound like a lawman."

Will nodded, reached in his pocket and showed his badge, then told Sweet about the beating and shooting in Twin Buttes.

When he finished Sweet said, "So that's it. I figured you fell down a mine shaft from the way you look."

Sweet thought a moment, then went on, "They live about three miles from here, down on Cottonwood Wash. Go straight south from here and when you hit the wash follow it east. When you come to the sorriest-, trashiest-looking place you've ever seen, that'll be it."

Will thanked him and they shook hands. Afterwards Will got his slicker from the saddle, shrugged into it and pulled his horse around. As he stepped into the rain, Sweet called, "You take care, hear?"

Will picked up the fence line and rode south through brown irrigated fields of alfalfa and finally reached piñon and cedar country. Cottonwood Wash was easy to find, for the cottonwoods, their yellow leaves now being stripped by the rain, loomed above the lower conifers.

When he reached the wide sandy wash he saw small rivulets that the rain had started. Although the sandy wash was easier traveling, he decided the last thing he wanted was to bog his horse down in quicksand, so he headed east on the bank of the wash. He came to a neat and well-kept set of adobe buildings, skirted them and continued on. The rain was coming down hard and steadily now, and Will guessed this country was in for a soaker.

Presently he broke from between two big dripping piñons, and what he saw made him rein up. Ahead of him, ringed by a scattering of piñon stumps, was a low and small mud-streaked, badly built shack. It had a dirt roof, its corners were uneven, the ridge pole sagged. Immediately around it, and between it and the log shed and corral, there was a litter of rusting bedsprings, a rotting mattress, a wheelless buckboard and a broken grindstone on a carpet of shattered glass from broken bottles. Weeds grew right up to the shack except where they were trampled underfoot. The whole scene bespoke neglect, indifference, and heedless poverty.

There was smoke coming from the rusty stovepipe of the shack, and Will guessed that at least one of the brothers was at home. He decided to circle the shack and approach it with the shed between it and him, thinking that the two glazed-paper windows were too dirty to see through.

He made his half-circle behind the screen of piñons, and when the shed was between him and the shack he dismounted, and tied his horse to a nearby tree. Afterwards he unbuckled his slicker so that his gun was within handy reach and then moved toward the shed. There was a lone, half-starved horse standing in the corral, his coat glistening with rain. His head was down and he did not even lift it to look at Will as he moved to the shed.

Above the sound of the rain pelting down on the side of the shed Will picked up a different sort of sound. It was a dim clang of metal on metal, followed by a man's rough cursing, and then the words, "You're already wet, God damn it! Now come out of there."

Will flattened against the side of the shed and waited until a man afoot and wearing a slicker, reins taut in one hand, tugged and yanked at the horse that reluctantly moved out into the rain.

Will brushed back his slicker, drawing his gun, and stepped out from his hiding place. The slight, bearded man saw him immediately. Gun hanging down from his hand, Will moved slowly toward the man and said flatly, "You're under arrest, McCartney."

"Not me. You got the wrong McCartney."

"Drop those reins and walk over here."

McCartney took a step and then swiftly dodged to the side of the horse, putting it between him and Will.

Then Will saw a slickered arm reach up over the horse's saddle and yank out a carbine from the saddle scabbard; it then disappeared over the saddle. Will heard the sound of a rifle being cocked. The carbine barrel appeared again and Will raised his six-gun and sighted it on the barrel, waiting. Abruptly the crown of a black hat appeared between the cantle and the horn of the saddle, and then the upper half of his face came into view. His arms were swinging the carbine

146

toward Will. Will shot at the half of the head he could see.

The arms disappeared and the carbine fell to the ground on Will's side of the saddle just as he heard the heavy splashing fall of McCartney's body.

He holstered his gun on the run, picked up the carbine and ran for McCartney's shack, cutting across the muddy barn lot for the door of the shack. He made it, went past it, and flattened himself against the shack wall. The door opened and a second man, shirtless and gun in hand, charged out the door for the shed.

Will lifted the carbine and called out, "Stop right there!"

The man halted, looked around and saw Will's carbine pointed at him.

"Drop it, or I'll shoot," Will said.

The man held a six-gun in his left hand, which meant he would have to turn his body to shoot. In the second it would take to turn and lift the gun he would be dead, and he realized it. Without moving anything except his fingers, he dropped the gun into the mud.

Will said, "Get back inside."

"But, my brother—" the man began.

Will cut in, "He's dead. Get back inside."

This McCartney, Will saw, was bigger than his brother, younger maybe, filthy and unshaven, with stringy blond hair down to his shoulders.

When he passed by Will, his body gave off the reek of a goat. Will, rifle in McCartney's back, followed him into a big room, the only room. A table with upended boxes for chairs stood against the wall; two canvas cots were at the far end, a small cast-iron stove was both kitchen stove and heater.

"Go sit down," Will said, "and keep your arms on the table."

McCartney moved over to a crate and did as he was told. Seated, he said, "Who are you?"

"We've met before," Will said. "Eight nights ago on the porch of the Mineral City Hotel."

Will watched as comprehension came into the slack-jawed face. Then the expression altered, and the man said sullenly, "I don't know what you're talking about."

Will raised the carbine waist high, pointed it and said, "Take off your belt and put it on the table."

"What for?"

Will cocked the carbine and shot, pointing the carbine so the bullet went over McCartney's forearms resting on the table. McCartney yanked his arms away and lunged to his feet. Will took a step backwards, levering a shell into the carbine. "Your belt," he said.

McCartney looked at him, his eyes bright with hatred, then he took off his wide leather belt and tossed it on the table.

"Back off," Will said. When McCartney moved away from the table Will went over and picked up the belt. Cradling the carbine in the crook of his left arm, he began to wrap the belt around his right fist.

The carbine pointed away from him, and knowing what was coming, McCartney lunged for Will. With half the belt around his fist, the buckle dangling, Will stepped back and took a vicious slash at McCartney's face. The buckle caught McCartney's cheek and raked across his nose and eyes. He halted abruptly, moaning, and raised both hands to his face.

Will took the carbine off cock, tossed it on the nearest cot, then finished wrapping the belt around his fist. McCartney still had his hands up, covering his face.

"I quit," he yelled.

"Not yet," Will said. He drove his belted fist at the exposed hinge of McCartney's jaw. The man went sprawling across the puncheon floor.

It was a beating. It was no fight from there on, and Will didn't intend it to be. Each time McCartney came to his feet, Will hit him with belted fist again and knocked him down. After three knockdowns McCartney stayed on his back, arms at his sides, his face bloody, his eyes open.

Will backed off and caught his breath, his anger ebbing. Presently he said, "Go sit down again."

McCartney staggered to his feet, lurched to one of the crates and sagged onto it, crossed his arms on the table and put his head on them.

Will took the marshal's badge from his pocket and laid it on the table in front of McCartney and said, "Look at this."

McCartney lifted his head and saw the badge, and said nothing. Will pocketed the badge and then sat down on the box opposite, his bloody fist still wrapped in the belt.

"McCartney, you're going to answer my questions, or get more of what you just got. Who paid you to beat me up?"

"I dun'no, I never seen him. He paid Riordan, and Riordan paid us." He was talking through cut and swelling lips.

With Riordan dead, there went any chance of identifying the man, Will thought bitterly. Or did it?

"Riordan must have told you something about him. What?"

"A city feller," McCartney said. "Leastways he had on town clothes and come out to Riordan's in a feed-stable buggy. He give Riordan two hundred dollars, and one hundred each for me and my brother. We was to get the same amount after we done the job of beatin' you up. Riordan wanted—"

"How'd you know where to find me?" Will interrupted.

"He told Riordan you'd be in Twin Buttes on the fifteenth."

Will frowned. He remembered they had telegraphed Magruder at the Mary E telling him to expect them on the 15th for the inspection of the Mary E. It was signed by Kevin as inspector. Was Magruder behind the beating?

Then he remembered that Magruder had sent Old Sam a telegram bitterly opposing the inspection. Magruder also sent a copy of his protest to Brady. Both telegrams mentioned the October 15th date. From his experience in the State House he knew the date would immediately be known to twenty men in the State House gang. It would also be known to every agent on the line.

"You started to say, 'Riordan wanted' —wanted what?"

McCartney thought a moment and said, "Riordan wanted to take the money and drift. He claimed this fellow would never pay us the other half. Why risk trouble when we already had money in our pockets?"

"What changed his mind?"

"Me and my brother did. We wanted the extra money."

"Why didn't he just go off alone?"

"He was afraid to. We'd worked with Riordan before. We told him if he drifted we'd go to the sheriff with what we knew. He'd be hunted all over the state. He was real sore about it."

"Was he still sore at you when you went up to Twin Buttes?"

"No, he'd went to town to check with the railroad people to see if any of them knew who it was that paid us. They did, and after that Riordan cooled off."

"What was the man's name? What did he do?"

McCartney shrugged. "We never asked and Riordan never told us. He just said he was good for the money."

Will sighed in quiet despair. Was this ignorant lout lying to him about not knowing the name of the man who had hired him?

He said, "You're going to spend a stretch of time in jail You might shorten that time if you could remember the name of the man that paid Riordan."

McCartney shook his head, his long hair falling across his face. "I don't know, I told you."

"Not even if you knew the man you shot at the hotel on the porch died of his wounds?"

"I never shot him," McCartney protested. "Bill did."

"I say you shot him. It's your word against mine. Guess who they'll believe?" Will paused. "Now, do you remember the name?"

McCartney clenched his fist and banged it down on the table. "I don't know, I tell you!" he shouted. "I could make up a name and give it to you, but I don't know!"

Will believed him. Again he sighed, and now he said, "No, you didn't shoot him; your brother did."

Will stood up. "Get your clothes on. I'm taking you and your brother to town."

He watched as the man shrugged into a filthy sheepskin coat. Only then did he realize he still had the belt around his hand. He took it off and tossed it to McCartney, who put it on.

Will crossed the room and picked up the carbine and waved McCartney to the door.

Out in the steadily falling rain they walked up to the other McCartney, who lay on his back in the mud.

Will halted his prisoner well away from the dead man, then moved over, searched the body, found the six-gun and threw it out in the bushes. Afterwards he called, "Come load him."

His face expressionless, the other McCartney came over. There was a hole in the forehead of the dead man, and the back half of his head was missing.

"Go get his horse," Will said. McCartney went to the shed where the horse had taken shelter out of the rain and led it up to the dead man.

Together they loaded the body across the saddle, belly down, and afterwards McCartney took the lariat from the horse's saddle and tied his brother's hands and feet together. Will pulled the skirt of the dead man's slicker over his head to hide the sight of it.

He waited for McCartney to saddle the other horse and put his rope around the neck of the led horse. Only then was Will aware of the sound of running water in Cottonwood Wash.

They headed for town, McCartney with the lead rope, and Will, carbine across his thighs, bringing up the rear.

They arrived in Hidalgo in mid-morning. Will was

151

drenched and shivering, and supposed McCartney was too. At the courthouse they tied the led horse to the tie rail and found the sheriff's office in the basement across from the four-celled jail. There were two men seated at desks as they entered, Will following McCartney with the carbine in his right hand. The older man looked at McCartney and said, "Oh, God, you again!" Then he looked at Will. "What is it this time, mister?"

Will took the badge from his pocket, moved over and laid it on the man's desk and said, "Name's Christie, Sheriff."

The sheriff rose and said, "Enright," and they shook hands.

"If you'll lock him up," Will said, "I'll tell you what this is all about. There's a dead man tied on a horse out front. That'll be his brother."

Sheriff Enright said to his young blond deputy, "Lock him up, Ernie. Then take the body over to the hardware store."

The deputy took down his slicker from a nail on the wall, shrugged into it, picked up the cell keys from his desk and motioned McCartney to come with him.

The sheriff moved over, closed the door, then came back to his desk. Sitting down, he reached for the bottom drawer and opened it, lifted out a bottle of whiskey and two glasses and poured two stiff drinks.

"You're shivering. I'm not, but a man shouldn't drink alone," he said.

Gratefully, Will, still standing, lifted the glass, made his thanks and drank half the contents. Afterwards he shrugged out of his slicker, pitched it against the wall, threw his carbine on it and then sat down in the chair facing the sheriff.

Enright seemed too young to warrant the grey in his hair. He had a square, stern face, bisected by a full black mustache. He was a big, muscular man with a flat belly that told Will he didn't spend much time sitting where he was now.

Enright, holding a pencil and pad in hand, had a look of patient curiosity as he waited for Will to begin.

"This starts a ways back," Will said. He began with his appointment as marshal to enforce mine inspections. He described the attack on the Mineral City Hotel porch in Twin Buttes, and the death of Riordan and the shooting of Kevin. After Kevin's death he said he was determined to track down the two men who were with Riordan. Then he told the happenings of this day: the help given him by Sweet, finding the place, and McCartney's attempt to shoot him, which resulted in the older brother's death.

When he had finished Enright looked thoughtfully at the wall over his desk, which held a dozen "Wanted" posters.

"That would make young McCartney an accessory to a murder, wouldn't it?"

"If you say so," Will said. "I'm so new at this job I don't know."

"This time we'll make it stick, and it'll be good riddance."

Both men finished their drinks, and then Will asked, "Anything holding me here?"

"I don't reckon," the sheriff said. "Your Kevin Lloyd was shot and later died in Granite Forks County, so they've got jurisdiction. My deputy will take McCartney to Twin Buttes and turn him over to Sheriff Thompson. As for your shooting of the other McCartney, that was purely self-defense. No, there's no reason you have to hang around."

Will rose, picked his slicker off the floor and leaned the carbine against the sheriff's desk. They shook hands, and Will, the slicker over his shoulder, mounted the stairs to street level.

After delivering his horse to the feed stable, he picked up his warbag and left the slicker. To get out of the rain he stepped into a nearly empty saloon, ordered a beer, took it over to one of the card tables and sat down.

On the way in with McCartney, he had given much

thought to the identity of the man who had paid Riordan. If Riordan, with his sorry background and probably limited intelligence, could track down the identity of the man who paid him, why couldn't he do the same thing? The problem was to find the brakeman Riordan had talked with, and the way to do that was to check with the agent here in Hidalgo.

He left his half-full glass of beer on the bar and headed across the muddy street for the depot.

The waiting room was empty, and the agent was seated behind the wicket by the sounder. He was listening but not writing. When he caught sight of Will he rose and came over to the counter, a man of middle age and stoop-shouldered, wearing black sleeve garters.

Will put his marshal's badge on the counter and asked mildly, "Wonder if you could help me?"

The agent picked up the badge, saw what it was and dropped it as if it had been hot.

"Why, sure, sure. What can I do for you?"

"Could you tell me how the brakemen are scheduled in and out of here?"

At the agent's puzzled look Will said, "I mean is it always the same brakeman who brings the train down from the north?"

"That's right. Ed Ruggles is his name. What did he do?"

Will smiled. "Not a thing. I just want to talk with him. Will he be on the train that goes out this afternoon?"

"Well, if he ain't, I'll sure be surprised," the agent said. "He brings it down from Twin Buttes, lays over eight hours and takes it back to Twin Buttes."

Will realized then he already knew Ed Ruggles, who, only this morning, had directed him to the café where he ate breakfast.

He asked, "He'll be on the three o'clock today?"

"Loading the bags," the agent said.

Will looked over the agent's shoulder at the big clock on the office wall and saw he had time enough to get something to eat. He thanked the man, put his warbag on the seat and went out into the diminishing rain.

He was finishing his coffee when he heard the engine making up in the yards, and he went back to the depot, where there were now a dozen passengers in the waiting room.

Presently the train pulled alongside the depot. Will picked up his warbag and filed with the others onto the platform. He waited until they were all aboard, and then halted by the brakeman waiting to toss the stepping stool onto the train.

Will said to him, "You're Ed Ruggles, the agent said."

At Ruggles' nod, Will gave his name and they shook hands.

Will said then, "When you're through taking tickets stop by my seat. I'd like to talk to you."

Ruggles looked puzzled, but he said, "Sure thing."

Will boarded, found an empty seat and in less than a minute the train began to roll out of the station. Ruggles came through the coach, lifted his ticket and went on to collect the others. When he was finished, he returned and sat down next to Will.

Ruggles was a man in his mid-thirties, Will judged, and he was wearing the same rough clothes as the rest of the train crew except for the visored cap that distinguished him from them. He had a broad, unweathered face with blue eyes, uptilted nose and the florid complexion of an Irishman.

Will said, "What I wanted to talk to you about happened some time around the first week in October. The man I'm interested in wore townsman's clothes and he was well dressed. He got off at Hidalgo, went over to the feed stable, hired a buggy and cut out east. That's about all I can tell you about him, because I got his description third-hand from a man who never saw him."

Ruggles frowned. "No age? No description?"

"My guess, and it's only a guess, is he'd be in his

forties. I think you'd notice him because he was dressed differently from most of the men who travel with you."

"A whiskey drummer, maybe? They like to dude it up."

"Maybe not so flashy," Will said.

Ruggles pondered this, and presently he shook his head. "I see a lot of people, but I can't remember anybody like that."

"All right. Maybe you'll remember this. A big, rough-looking man, dirty and needing a shave worse than I do, asked you about him in Hidalgo. He probably talked with you on the platform."

Ruggles turned his head and looked at Will with surprise. "I remember him—a redhead?"

"I don't know," Will said.

"I know the man he was asking about."

"Know him, or remember him?" Will asked.

"I remember him. He works for this railroad. The reason I know is because he showed me his pass."

"Remember his name on the pass?"

"Sure. We don't get many people on a pass. He was from Congress Junction and the name on the pass was Eric Reynolds. We talked railroad a while."

Will felt a leap of his heart. "Did the redhead say why he wanted to know Reynolds' name?"

"No, he didn't. I didn't tell him his name either. I just said he worked for us."

"That's what I wanted to know," Will said. "I'm much obliged to you, too."

"Hope it helps," Ruggles said, and rose. "See you later."

He went forward in the car, and Will reflected on the information Ruggles had given him. He now had the name of the man who had paid Riordan, but who had sent Reynolds down here to hire Riordan and the McCartneys to beat them up?

Obviously, if Reynolds knew the date that he and Kevin would be in Twin Buttes he must have been told by Magruder, Hatcher or one of the railroad agents.

156

But the money involved was eight hundred dollars—a sum that only a rich man could offer.

Immediately Will connected the amount of money with the fact that Reynolds rode on a pass which Frank Jackson had signed.

The Rocky Mountain Central had already made, and was making, a fortune from the mines. Had these mines, fearing the additional cost of inspections, gone to Jackson to ask him to act as go-between? Had Jackson ordered Reynolds to find the hardcases for his beating? Was the beating the mine owners' way of scaring him and Kevin off?

Nothing else made sense. Reynolds had been sent down to find a relative of one of the rustlers who had been killed in the Tres Piedras battle. When he was identified, that automatically exonerated the mine owners, since it was obviously an act of a man out for personal revenge.

In other words, Frank Jackson was indirectly responsible for Kevin's death. The anger of yesterday was back with him. When he got to Granite Forks, he would hunt down Jackson and make him give him the facts.

It was close to dusk when the train pulled into the Granite Forks depot. Will was the first passenger off.

The new brakeman—not Ruggles, who had left the train at Twin Buttes—was standing at the foot of the steps. Giving Will a smile, he asked, "Good trip?"

"Couldn't have been better."

"That's because it was uphill all the way. See you again sometime."

Will headed for the line of hacks. He had already thought of his next move. Chances were that at this hour Jackson would be at the Granite Forks House bar, where he could talk politics with and buy drinks for the legislators who stopped there.

He threw his warbag into the closest hack, climbed in and told the driver to take him to the Granite Forks

House. As the driver backed his rig around and swung in a half-circle to go into Front Street, Will looked over the driver's shoulder and saw that the second-floor corner room of the brick building ahead of him was lamplit. This, he recalled, was Frank Jackson's office. Since there were no lamps lit in the anteroom that housed his secretaries, he assumed that Frank was alone. He ordered the driver to pull up on the side street by the wrought-iron staircase. When the hack stopped he asked the driver to wait and started up the stairs. Frank might have someone with him but that didn't matter a damn.

Will reached the landing, opened the corridor door and knocked on the heavy wooden door to his right. A voice inside called something but it was muffled by the thickness of the door, and Will knocked again.

The door opened, throwing a shaft of lamplight into the corridor and Will saw Jackson silhouetted against the room's light. Beyond it, Will saw that Jackson had been seated at the round table, his drink on it and papers scattered over it.

"Hello, Will," Jackson said easily. "Heard you were out of town. Come in."

"Hello, Frank. Saw the light in your window and hoped I'd find you."

"Yes, I had some late work for the conference hearing tomorrow," Frank said. He closed the door. "I'm having a lonesome drink, will you join me?"

"Not now, thanks. Maybe later." Privately Will thought, *I'll be damned if I'd drink with an enemy.*

"Sit down, Will," Frank said appraising him. "God, you look beat."

"I know," Will said.

He went over to the table, tossed his hat on it, and then instead of sitting in the chair he sat on one of its wide arms and watched Jackson seat himself.

Jackson reached for his drink. "What's on your mind, Will?"

"Kevin Lloyd is dead," Will said.

Frank frowned. "He was your partner on the in-

158

spection trip, wasn't he?" At Will's nod, he said, "I hadn't heard. I'm sorry, Will."

"You should be," Will said bluntly. "You are responsible for his death."

Jackson put down his drink and said in a tone of quiet surprise, "What in God's name are you talking about?" His lean face seemed to hold genuine puzzlement.

"Does the name Eric Reynolds mean anything to you?"

A subtle change came over Jackson's face. He frowned and said, "Not at the moment. Why?"

"You signed a pass for him. Can't you remember who you give passes to? If it'll help, his address is Congress Junction."

"Oh, yes, I do remember now. Tall, good-looking fellow."

"What was he doing down in Hidalgo three weeks ago?"

Frank frowned. He reached for his drink, took a sip and said, "If I've got the right man, and I think I have, he's an inspector for our finance office." He shrugged then. "Not all of our agents are completely honest, Will. They'll work with the brakemen—"

"I don't give a damn about the railroad's problems," Will interrupted. "Let's stick to Eric Reynolds."

"I was trying to," Jackson said stiffly. "What I'm saying is, he travels all over. Why not Hidalgo?"

"Because he rented a buggy there, rounded up three hardcases and gave them four hundred dollars to beat me up in Twin Buttes on the fifteenth."

Jackson's face was stony now as he said, "I doubt it. Can you prove it? Did anybody see him give these men money?"

"The only man who saw it is dead," Will said. "I think you know that already. It was in the *Herald*."

"Oh, yes. His name was Riordan, the man who had a grudge against you for three years." He frowned and when he spoke again the same coldness was in his voice. "What's this got to do with me, Will? Why are you telling me this?"

"Because the money Reynolds paid them came from you."

"Once more, can you prove it in court?"

"No. I won't have to," Will said. "This is the court."

"Does your court accept only hearsay circumstantial evidence? No other court does." He finished his drink and held the glass in his hand. "It wouldn't even accept what I'm about to tell you. You're the only witness and I'll deny I said it."

"Said what?"

"Sure, I paid Reynolds to have those hardcases beat you up," Jackson said calmly. "I told 'em no shooting, just a beating. You're getting a helluva lot too big for your britches. It's time you were cut down to size."

Through his new anger Will could scarcely believe what he had heard. "Mining money?" he asked in a choked voice.

"No, my money," Jackson said. "You beat up a friend of mine for no cause at all. I had you beat up for him. You're too big for him to handle."

"That would be Costigan," Will said flatly.

At Jackson's nod Will asked, "Your idea or his?"

"Let's say we had a meeting of minds," Jackson said.

Now Jackson rose, held up his glass and said, "Can I fix you one?"

Will shook his head as Jackson started for the liquor cabinet in the corner. Will sat for stunned seconds trying to understand what he had just heard. Kevin had died because Costigan and Jackson thought Will should be taught a lesson.

He came off the chair arm, whirled, took two steps and lunged at Jackson's back. His shoulder drove into him and Jackson catapulted forward head-first into the glass doors of the big cabinet, which shattered at contact with his head. Jackson cursed, dropped his glass, pulled his shoulder away from the cabinet and reached down for a drawer under the bar space and yanked it open.

Will was on his back then, his hand streaking for Jackson's wrist, which had almost reached the gun lying in the drawer. Will wrapped his left arm around Jackson's middle and heaved him back from the cabinet and the gun. In a slow but savage effort, he twisted Jackson's right arm behind his back. Jackson cried out with pain as Will pressed his feet to the floor and lifted his arm in an ever-tightening hammerlock. Jackson, yelling with pain, tried to stomp Will's feet. Implacably, Will kept lifting on the hammerlock until Jackson was on tiptoe, trying in desperation to ease the pain.

And then came Jackson's scream. Will heard and felt the muscles in Jackson's shoulder give with the muted tearing sound of bone and gristle parting. Will felt Jackson's body slack, and through his seething rage he realized that Jackson had fainted. He let go of him and he sank to the floor, falling on his face. Jackson's right arm, incapable of any movement, still remained in a grotesque position behind his back.

Will stood over him, breathing great lungfuls of air as he looked down at him.

Afterwards, when he had caught his breath, he went out of the room by way of the corridor, leaving the door open.

26

Next morning, after Will had cleaned up and had breakfast at the hotel, he went immediately to Brady Cope's house. He knew he would be too late to catch

Brady at home, but he was fairly certain he would find Belle there. He told himself that Belle would surely know if the files had been examined, and what they held. That was only partly true; he just wanted to see Belle.

He rang, but the doorbell was not answered immediately, and then he heard from inside the house footsteps hurrying down the stairs.

When Belle opened the door the instant look of disbelief vanished. She smiled and said, "Oh, Will!" and stepped up to him holding out her arms. Will, surprised, raised his arms and hugged her, and she kissed him on the cheek.

"Where have you been?" she asked. "I've been worried sick about you. You could have telegraphed us."

"The telegram would have been a yard long. Besides, I had no time to send it."

A certain reserve came into Belle's face, as if she regretted her impetuosity in kissing him, or so Will read it.

Belle said, "Come in," and led the way into the living room. Will closed the door behind him and watched Belle turn and look into his eyes.

"You got in on last night's train?" she asked.

At Will's nod she said, "That was six-thirty last night. It's ten o'clock now. You couldn't have been in much of a hurry to see us, Will."

Will turned and sat down on the sofa. He patted the cushion next to him as an invitation for her to sit beside him. Instead, Belle ignored the gesture and sat down in the easy chair facing the sofa.

"The spirit was willing, Belle, but the old body wasn't. I went to my room, fell across the bed and didn't wake up until long past daylight. Oh, yes, I did one other thing before I went home. I broke Frank Jackson's shoulder."

Belle's lips parted in surprise. "You what? Why?"

Either Belle had forgotten her disappointment with him, or her curiosity was consuming, because she rose,

162

came over to him and sat down on the cushion next to his, half facing him.

"What does that mean, Will?"

"Kevin died. I found that Frank Jackson paid those roughnecks to beat me up." He paused. "I'll start at the beginning."

He told then of the ride from Millerton to Twin Buttes and of going directly to Doc Kelly's house. The doctor, returning from calls, had found Kevin dead, probably of apoplexy. It was only then, Will told her, that he realized that what had started as a scuffle was now murder, premeditated or not, and he was determined to find the man who caused Kevin's death.

Looking at Belle, Will saw the tears streaming down her cheeks. She wiped them away, and as Will patted her on the knee he said, "Strange how the old boy got to everyone who knew him."

Belle nodded. "What did you do, Will?"

Will told of going down to Hidalgo and of getting information at the horse ranch that tied in the McCartneys with the dead Riordan. The killing of one brother, the whipping of the other, he related only briefly. The nameless, faceless man who had paid off Riordan and whom Riordan had checked on with the brakeman at Hidalgo was only hearsay evidence.

By now, Belle was listening so intently that she did not notice when Will removed his hand from her knee.

Meeting the brakeman whom Riordan had talked to was a bit of blind luck, as Will described it. When the name of the man and the fact that he carried a pass signed by Jackson were connected, it pointed straight to Frank Jackson. Will told then of going to Jackson's office straight from the depot, and of how Jackson, cornered, had admitted his man had paid Riordan and the other two for the Twin Buttes beating. Jackson had pointed out to Will that he had no case in court, since the only man who could testify against him or his messenger was dead.

Will admitted losing his head then when he realized this man, originally responsible for Kevin's death, would go scot free. Jackson even declared that the beating in Twin Buttes was in retaliation for Will's beating of Costigan. Again, unprovable in court.

Will said he charged Jackson then, kept him from his gun and put a hammerlock on him that broke his shoulder.

"How do you know that, Will?" Belle asked.

Will hesitated. "I heard it give."

Belle shivered. Will ended by saying, "That's why I didn't come over last night, Belle. The hack driver had to wake me up at my house."

Belle rose and without a word went into the kitchen. Will heard the sound of the sink pump working. Presently she returned. She had washed away the tear-stains from her face but they still marked the bodice of her forest-green dress. This time Belle sat down beside him without having to be invited.

She took his hand and said, "I'm sorry I was so selfish, Will. I guess we're pretty lucky to have you here at all. Aside from missing you, we need you now. This very afternoon."

"That's good to know, but for what?"

"Pa, Joe and Jim are meeting with Old Sam and Frank Jackson this afternoon. Pa put it off as long as he could because you were missing. Now you're here. Pa will go in there with all the artillery there is."

"The files?"

Belle nodded, and then proceeded to tell him what the files had revealed.

The fifty-odd damaging letters they had sorted from the bulk of the files all indicated solicitation and receipt of bribes. Twenty-two were actionable in court.

A good number of these were written by Evans at Old Sam's request and were initialed by him. Belle herself had made copies of these letters while Brady and Joe had prepared the indictment.

Will listened to her with growing excitement. At

long last they had Old Sam and his machine backed into a corner.

"How's Brady going to use these letters, Belle?"

"He and Joe will be home in an hour. I'll let them tell you, Will."

She squeezed his hand that she held and said, "It's pretty wonderful, isn't it?"

Will only nodded, smiling to himself. Belle withdrew her hand and said, "Let's heat up some coffee for us."

She went into the kitchen and Will trailed her. He watched her stir up the fire and add wood to it. Her every movement held a grace for him he couldn't explain. He remembered their rides together before all this heartbreak had started. Looking back now, he knew that even then he wanted to marry her. At the time he'd been Joe Isom's idle clerk, directionless and impatient, with no prospect of change in sight. Although they had liked each other then, he knew he was a damned poor prospect for any girl to take for a husband.

Well, what was different now? For one thing, they had worked together for a purpose, learning to know each other better and relying on each other. For another, Old Sam could never survive the ordeal he would have to face. If he elected to fight he would be driven out of office by public opinion. That meant that Joe Isom would take over as Governor and Will would be Joe's right hand. That was something. Belle had watched this evolve.

He said, "Come here, Belle," then thought, *What a helluva spot to propose—in the kitchen.*

Belle came over to him and he put his big hands on her slender shoulders. He said quietly, watching her eyes, "Have I ever told you that you're a damned beautiful woman and I'm in love with you?"

Belle blushed and said gently, "Not in words, but in other ways, yes."

He drew her to him and they kissed, and then he put his arms around her.

165

Will said into her ear, "Then, why in hell don't we do something about it, like get married?"

Belle whispered into his ear, "Yes, why the hell don't we?"

27

Brady's and Joe's appointment with Old Sam was set for two in the afternoon. Will as Joe's secretary and Jim as Brady's secretary would be present. Brady had asked that Frank Jackson also be invited.

Brady, with Jim carrying his briefcase, picked up Will and Joe at Joe's office and then went next door into the big anteroom of the Governor's suite. They were shown immediately into the Governor's office by Ed Poland, Old Sam's older secretary. Old Sam left the papers he was fiddling with at his desk and came over to greet them—a big, friendly bear of a man who shook hands all around. Frank Jackson, seated in a chair facing Old Sam's desk, his right arm immobile in a sling of clean white cloth, waved his left arm—a greeting which did not include Will.

Old Sam gestured toward the big oblong conference table surrounded by eight leather-covered straight-backed conference chairs. On the table in front of each was a pad and pencils. Brady circled the desk and stood back of the chair on Old Sam's left. Joe took the chair next to him and put the briefcase on the table. Looking over the rest of the people now in the room as Old Sam made for his seat, Brady noticed another secretary and—surprisingly—Jimmy Day, who smiled at him. Frank Jackson moved up to a chair on Old Sam's right and the three secretaries moved to the chairs down the table from Jackson.

Old Sam seated himself, which was a signal for the others to do likewise, except for Brady, who still stood with his hands on the back of his chair, until Old Sam looked at him quizzically.

"Sam, do you need all of your people with us?" Brady asked.

Old Sam frowned slightly. "Well, this meeting ought to be recorded. What about your people?"

"They already know what we'll be talking about, Sam. For your sake I don't think your people should."

"That's an odd thing to say," Sam growled, watching him.

"It's an odd situation. Bear with me, will you?"

Sam looked around and said, "We've all got pads and pencils, Ed. So why don't you fellows leave us."

Brady sat down as the three men left the room and closed the door behind them.

"Want me to start?" Brady asked.

At Sam's sober nod of assent, Brady said, "As you all know by now, we're back in possession of Hugh Evans' party files."

Old Sam took a deep breath and said, "You don't lack for nerve, do you, Brady?"

"No," Brady admitted. "I might add that since the files were unlocked we went through them."

"Would you have gone through them if they'd been locked?" Frank Jackson asked, an edge of temper in his voice.

"Most assuredly I would have," Brady said.

"Find anything new?" Old Sam asked.

"Not to you, but new to me," Brady answered. He looked down his side of the table to Jim, who opened the briefcase, took out some papers and handed them to Joe, who in turn handed them to Brady.

"I have here," Brady said, "evidence that Hugh Evans not only solicited, but accepted bribes in your

167

behalf and at your request, Sam." He looked at Frank Jackson. "The new state party chairman was one who asked for favors and got them and paid you handsomely."

Old Sam growled, "Let me have a look at what you've got."

Brady handed him the papers, saying, "These are copies, Sam. I'm holding the originals for evidence in court."

The Governor looked at only half a dozen of the copies and wordlessly handed them to Frank Jackson. They were all silent as Frank put the papers on the desk and leafed through them with his good hand. When he had finished he said, "May we keep these?"

"Of course."

"What do you propose doing, Brady?" Frank asked.

"Why, call a special grand jury, of course. I expect to get an indictment on at least twenty-two counts. Those you have in your hands."

Frank leaned back, looked at Brady and said, "You expect to make a deal or you wouldn't have called for this appointment. What is it you want?"

Brady shifted. "I want Sam's resignation as Governor before Christmas. It'll be for reasons of health. That'll give him a chance to miss a lot of appointments. At those he keeps he will complain to everyone about the state of his health."

Now he looked at Jackson, who was observing Isom.

Jackson said, "So Joe can step into the Governorship?"

"That's what our State Constitution says, isn't it?"

Jackson looked at him with undisguised hatred. "Then, no grand jury?" Frank asked.

"Not if Sam steps out," Brady answered.

"What else?" Frank demanded.

"You, Frank, are to resign as party chairman. You are to move your office up to Congress Junction. You're the Central's vice president and you can arrange it easily. I'd like to get you as far away from the Capitol as possible. And still keep you in the state so I don't have to extradite you."

Jackson's face flushed with anger. "You're the czar, so I'm being sent to Siberia. Is that it?"

"Not quite," Brady said calmly. "Czars execute assassins, and you're an assassin, Frank."

"That's a damned lie!" Jackson said hotly.

Brady went on calmly, "You paid three men to beat up Will in Twin Buttes. One of your men was killed. Kevin Lloyd died as a result of a wound inflicted by your men. If you'd like your guilt or innocence to be judged by a jury I can arrange a trial. I repeat, you're an assassin."

Jackson's face was livid. He looked at Will and then away from him, picked up one of the indictments, read it and glanced at Old Sam.

The Governor's face still expressed both surprise and shock. He was silent for long moments, and then he asked, "Is that true, Frank?"

"I'll explain it later, Sam."

From down the table Will said, "I'll explain it now, Governor." When Old Sam's attention was fixed on him, he went on. "He was doing a favor for your mutual friend, Phil Costigan. I beat up Phil for printing lies about me in the *Herald*. He asked Frank to hire some bullyboys to beat me up. They did. Brady told you the rest."

"Where did you get this information?" Old Sam asked.

"From Frank last night. Why do you think his arm is in a sling?"

Old Sam didn't answer and neither did Frank, who was studying the indictment.

"Are we finished, Brady?" Old Sam asked in a tone of voice that was suddenly weary.

"Not quite," Brady said. "Under the new Mining Commission law you have the power to appoint five members from each party to the new Mining Commission. Don't make any appointments before you retire, Sam. Leave those appointments to Joe."

169

Old Sam nodded that he had heard.

"Another thing, Sam. You gave orders out to swing all the state's printing to Phil Costigan. Cancel those orders."

"But he's the only printer in town," Sam objected.

"By Christmas the *Herald* will be for sale," Brady answered.

There was a long silence, and then Sam said, "I want to hear you say it again, Brady. If I do all the things you want, you won't call up a grand jury?"

"That's my promise," Brady said, "provided you do one more thing."

Old Sam watched him, wondering what was coming.

"Turn back all those Mary E stock certificates that Hugh Evans signed over to you. That would make a conflict of interests court case that would go down in history."

There was real shock in Old Sam's face as he listened to what Brady said. Then he asked, "May I ask how you knew about them?"

"You may ask, but I won't answer," Brady replied.

Brady rose now, about to say, "Thank you, gentlemen," but he did not say it.

Instead, he only said, "Thank you."